THE OREGON TERRITORY

THE RETURN OF TRAVIS WALKER - BOOK THREE

DAVE P. FISHER

Published by DS Productions

ISBN: 9798399405889

FOREWORD

Merriam-Webster describes a trilogy as: *a series of three dramas or literary works that are closely related and develop a single theme.*

The Return of Travis Walker is a three-part journey of three men, whose lives have been severely altered by the crimes of other men. Travis, the murder of his sons by the Cheyenne Indians. Martin, by the barbaric destruction of his family. Prisque, who returned to his true name of Nicholas, being taken as an orphaned boy, and forced into a life of crime. They, by varying circumstances, all come together for one common goal, to render justice on the men who tore apart their lives. Thus, the journey begins.

The Return of Travis Walker is a, single-themed, life-changing journey for these men. It was not written to be three distinct adventure tales, but one continuous story, set in three parts. Each novel ends with the men realizing they have to change their plans and direction, but not entirely sure how, but going on all the same. The next novel picks up that new direction, revealing the changing attitudes, questions, and growth along the way. They encounter obstacles they must overcome, and in doing so, their education, understanding, and goals shift.

Ending one element of the journey, then taking up the next element, is part of a single-themed trilogy. There *are* *no* conclusions until the journey is completed. The questions, and future, are still suspended in the air, they have no answers for the questions. This third novel completes their journey, and by it, they are stronger mentally, and emotionally, then from their start.

Rather than looking at The Return of Travis Walker, as three independent adventure novels, with all the threads tied off at the end of each. The threads cannot be tied off because the journey has not ended. I would hope you see this work as an ongoing study of the human spirit to overcome tragedy and obstacles. To seek justice where none existed, and how time changes everything. On top of that, you will receive a geography, and history lesson.

Thank you for reading,
Dave

1

Travis and Martin stood; their eyes locked on Prisque for a silent moment of revelation. Only the hoots from a pair of owls broke the still of the night. The moon shone down on Prisque, casting him in a surrealistic glow, and highlighting the glistening blood of the men he had just slain. It was a moment of telling, a surprise to Martin, but an answer to Travis' suspicions.

Travis broke the silent standoff, "What should we call you now? Prisque, or Nicolas?"

"Nick," he replied. "My father always called me Nick, I prefer it. I've lived under my false name long enough. I am Nick Dupre."

The shock began to clear from Martin's mind as he came to grips with the fact, that all was changed in what he *thought* he knew about his friend. "I have so many questions, Prisque – Nick."

Nick looked at him, "I know. I hope I can answer them all for you."

"The most important question I have is, "Were you involved with that night?"

"No, Martin. I swear to you, I was not. If I had known what they were going to do, I would have killed them before they got to you."

Martin studied Nick, then slowly nodded his acceptance of the answer, "I believe you."

"Thank you." Nick shifted his attention to Travis, "You knew, didn't you?"

"I suspected you were not Prisque Trembly, as you claimed. You seemed to know too much about the outlaws. The fact you always found a reason to be away when we confronted them, told me something as well."

"I couldn't have them identify me in front of you, not before I could kill Duncan Black."

Martin frowned at Travis, "You knew, and you did not tell me?"

Travis turned his eyes to Martin, "I suspected, but I was not about to make an accusation I couldn't support. If I was wrong, I didn't want to set you against your friend on my suspicions."

Martin considered Travis' explanation for a moment, then said, "You are right. It would have been wrong to say that on suspicion alone. Now, we know the truth for certain." He looked back at Nick, "I would like to know everything, from the beginning."

"You deserve that," Nick replied. "It will take some time, there is a lot to tell."

"We can go back to the camp and talk," Martin said.

Nick shook his head, "This is nothing the rest need to hear, it is for the ears of the two of you only."

"Fair enough," Travis said.

"Yes, that is fair," Martin agreed.

"We should get away from these dead men," Nick remarked.

"Yeah, it's not the best settin' for a long talk," Travis said.

"What of them?" Martin asked. "They will be found."

"At the end of rendezvous, it's not uncommon to find dead men," Travis replied. "Men fight, old scores are settled. The trappers know we were lookin' for these murderers, and will probably figure we found 'em, and nothin' more will be said."

"What of their stolen pelts?" Martin asked.

"I'll give them to Jim, he can sell them with the others," Travis answered.

Taking the reins to their horses, they walked down the stream leading the animals. A quarter mile from the outlaw's camp, and clear of the noise of the rendezvous, they came to several dead trees lying by the water. Tying their horses to the willows, they sat on the logs, Nick on one, facing Travis and Martin on one opposite him.

Away from the commotion of the outlaw camp, the chirping chorus of crickets, and little peeper frogs filled the night, aside from them, it was a quiet place. The moon reflected off the moving water, and illuminated the hot July night. Nick sat gathering his thoughts, as Travis and Martin waited for him to start.

"I was born, and grew to fourteen years of age, in the Newcastle District of Rupert's Land, on the shores of Balsam Lake. My father's name was Gabriel, he was a trapper, a coureur, who refused to pay tribute to Hudson's Bay. They tried to catch him, but he knew the woods too well for them, and he was never caught. He was forty years old when I was born. He taught me to trap, live in the woods, and to despise Hudson's Bay.

"One winter, when I was twelve years of age, we were crossing the ice on a lake when the ice broke, and he plunged in. He never came back up. It is easy to be lost under the ice, and finding the hole you fell through is sometimes impossible before you freeze in the water, and drown – as my father did.

"My father had an older brother, Antoine. They had grown up in the woods together, their father, my grandfather, was a trapper and trader. As adults, Antoine often left Balsam Lake, be gone for a time, then return. My father was always at odds with his brother, but he never said what the problem was between them. I once heard my father trying to talk him into changing something, but I didn't know what that was. Antoine left one day, and didn't return. After my father's death, my mother told me that Antoine was a river pirate, that was why he went away, to return to piracy, and that was the problem father had with him. She said it was a family secret, and I was never to tell a soul that Uncle was a villainous river pirate. So, you see, I was telling you the truth about that."

Travis nodded, "Yes, you said that. I believed you, but suspected there was a lot more to the story."

Nick nodded, "There was. It made sense to me then, what father was trying to turn him away from. My father was considered an outlaw by the corrupt Hudson's Bay officials, but he was an entirely honest, and good man. He was disgusted that his brother was an outlaw, worse yet, a pirate. Two years after my father was lost to the lake, my mother died. It was difficult to be fourteen years old, and fending for yourself, but I tried.

"A month later, Antoine returned to the cabin to see father. When he learned that he, and my mother were dead, he left and took me with him. I knew he was an outlaw, but being an orphaned child, I didn't have much of a choice. Fend for myself, or go with my uncle.

"Antoine introduced me to his pirate gang, those we killed out here, were part of that gang I grew up with. They began to train me. Antoine proved to be a brutal trainer. He would teach me a lesson in stealing, or fighting, and if I didn't get it right, he would beat me. If I cried from it, he would tie me to a tree all night. He said, I was soft as a rabbit's ear, and he was going to make me tough.

"The others treated me the same, until I became stronger and tougher than them. By eighteen, I was a hardened pirate, skilled in weapons, and had grown calloused to death, as we killed men for their goods. At that age, the man who was second in command of the gang, punched me for refusing to address him as, *sir*. I killed him with my knife, and Antoine made me second in command. No one ever hit me again."

"Which explains why killin' those Indians was not unsettlin' for you," Travis remarked.

Nick nodded, "Killing men, who are trying to kill me, means nothing to me."

"How much longer did you stay with them?" Martin asked.

"Three more years. One night, we attacked a merchant's boat, and killed the three men on it. Going into the owner's cabin on the boat, I saw a portrait of three women on the wall. I held my lantern up to see it better. It was a woman, and two young girls. Written at the bottom were the words, 'my beloved ladies'. I stared at the portrait and felt my heart tear, we had killed that man. He would never return to his beloved ladies again. I could feel their tears, and grief, and my hand was the cause.

"I'm not sure what did it, or if I was finally coming to some manner of morality, but I was suddenly overcome with grief, and sick at heart, for what I had done. My father, who I loved so much, his face rose before my eyes, and his eyes and mouth held the same disgusted look he gave his brother. I had broken his heart, and shamed his name. I walked off that boat, and never went back. I kept going until I was deep in the woods, and there I wept for my accursed life, and shame. After that, I took up the traplines, and tried to forget the wretchedness of my past. I forever, to this day, see the faces of 'my beloved ladies.'"

Martin looked at his friend with sadness in his eyes, "Is that what you saw in Colette, and my daughters? That man's wife and daughters?"

Nick looked into Martin's eyes, "Yes. I hoped that by giving them my love, and friendship, I would somehow make recompense for my crimes, and what I had done to 'my beloved ladies.'"

"You brought them gifts, each time you visited."

"I liked to do that. Colette was like a sister to me, and the girls, my nieces. I loved them all, for I had no one."

"Then, those same pirates murdered them," Martin said softly.

Nick tensed his jaws, and stared at the stream for a long moment, "Yes, and I vowed they would die for it."

"How did you know, it was them?" Martin asked.

"After five years, I decided I wanted more than living in the woods, and staying ahead of the Hudson Bay agents."

"You seemed to know the workin's of the Hudson Bay agents, pretty well," Travis said.

"If you want to stay ahead of your enemy, it is best to learn all you can about how they work. My father had taught me some about them, but later, I knew a coureur who had been a Bay agent, and he told me everything about their politics and dirty tricks. That is why I know so much about them."

Travis nodded, "Like we do here with the Indians."

"Same thing. That's why I ask so many questions about the Indians. I want to know my enemy, or if they are friends. Anyway, I headed down the Mississippi River, coming to St. Louis. The fur market was booming, and after having sold pelts for years to buyers who made a better profit than me, without half of the work, I decided to become a fur buyer. I changed my name to Prisque Trembly, if anyone knew the reputation of Antoine and Nicholas Dupre, they would never do business with me, or the law would be on me. I bought a small shop, and I had some money to invest, so I became Prisque Trembly, fur buyer."

"It is a difficult trade you chose, very fickle," Martin remarked.

Nick nodded, "So, I found out. I made some profit, but it was nerve-wracking wondering if I would make my money back, especially when I was competing with the big fur houses from the East."

"I met you at the first auction you attended," Martin said. "You looked confused, so I thought I should help you."

"Yes, I was very confused as to how it all worked. It was much more complicated than I had thought. I was appreciative of your help."

"We became friends," Martin added.

"Yes, we did. I learned a lot from you, and began to show a profit. I was never up to your level, but I was doing well enough."

Martin smiled, "My level is far below that of Rene Auguste and Jean Pierre Chouteau."

"Perhaps, but you are a good trader," Nick replied.

"What happened to bring Duncan Black into it all?" Travis asked.

"One day, Antoine brought a man with a bright red beard and hair into the gang. He introduced him as Duncan Black, and he stepped right in like he owned the gang. He was bold and belligerent. The rest of the gang resented him. He stayed clear of me, though, I think because Antoine told him who I was, and to leave me be. He was a wretched scoundrel, worse than the others. He especially liked to rape the women. I found that vile, and it was the main reason I came to hate him. Attacking men, was one thing, but what he did to women was beyond the pale. Several of the gang fell in with him in doing it. Antoine never stopped them."

"I later remembered Duncan Black from the Red River Colony," Martin said. "He was a villain, and did the bidding of his Bay masters. I have no idea what Antoine looks like, but, if I saw him, I might remember him."

"You won't ever see him now. I had been in St. Louis a year before meeting you, Martin. So, it was four years before the gang showed up in St. Louis. When I heard that Brian Harper had been murdered and robbed of his pelts, I wondered if it was a random attack, or had the gang worked its way south. Then, people were saying that a red bearded man was the leader of a gang of thieves and murderers, and I knew it was them.

"A few days after Harper's murder, Antoine and Black came into my shop with the stolen pelts. They were as shocked to see me, as I was to see them. It was a meeting, I hoped to never have, and there the two wretches stood, their arms full of stolen pelts. After their initial shock at seeing me wore off, they acted like they were happy to see me. They wanted me to buy their pelts. I refused. I told them, I knew they had murdered Brian Harper for the pelts, and to take them, and get out. They did not take that well, but they left.

"A couple of days later, the auction was being held. You came to it, we met, and I saw you were upset. When you told me, two men, one with a red beard, had sold pelts to you, and you were worried about them, because you suspected he was someone you had known. That's when I began to worry because Duncan Black had been to your house. When you mentioned they had seen Colette. That's when I told you to go home as fast as you could. I was hoping they had only sold you the pelts that I wouldn't buy, but Black was a man not to be trusted in the slightest, especially if women were involved.

"I got our pelts into the auction, then went out looking for Antoine and Black. I expected to find them in a tavern, I knew of a few where scoundrels hung out. The second one I checked, I found them. I confronted Antoine, and told him I knew that Black had sold pelts to Martin Ouimette. I knew how they were, and if anything happened to Martin, or especially the girls, I would gut him like a deer. They had better stay away from you, and your family."

"How did they respond to that?" Martin asked.

"Antoine said he had no interest in you, that you were just someone to sell the pelts to, since I wouldn't buy them. Then, they tried to get me to come back in with them, or at least buy any future pelts they had. I told them, no. Antoine said, that I owed him, for all he had done for me. I had some choice words for him, as to what I *owed* him. I gave them a final warning to leave you alone.

"The next morning, Antoine came to the shop alone. He apologized to me for how he had acted, and asked me to come to breakfast with him, just as uncle and nephew, no one else. He wanted to talk about my father, and what had happened to him. I agreed, and went with him to the same tavern. It was stupid of me to have trusted him, but when he said he wanted to talk about father, I went with him."

"I'm sure that didn't go well," Travis said. "What happened?"

"He must have arranged it with the barmaid, to put something in my drink or food, because I found myself growing drowsy as we talked. The next thing I realized, there was a hand in the inside pocket of my coat. I came suddenly awake to find the barmaid with her hand in my pocket trying to snitch my purse. I grabbed her arm, and she went into a frenzy, clawing and punching me. I let go of her arm, she raked my face again, then she ran out the door. I felt for my purse and it was still there, then I looked across the table to see that Antoine was gone. He had done something, but I didn't know what it was, or how long I had been out."

"That was the squaw claws on your face, and black eye," Travis said. "She got both hands free, that's how she got both sides of your face."

Nick nodded, "You thought it was something else. That I couldn't possibly have marks on both sides of my face, if I had one of her arms. It's understandable."

"I apologize for assuming you were lying," Travis said.

Nick shrugged, "No harm done."

"When did you find out what had happened?" Martin asked.

"That same day. I knew Antoine had done something, why he drugged me, I didn't know at the time, but I soon figured out why."

"The jewelry," Travis said.

Nick looked at him, "How did you know?"

"The way the pouch was thrown under the bush, right next to the coins, and your horse tracks by it. If it had fallen from an outlaw's torn pocket, it wouldn't have landed *under* the bush."

Nick huffed a laugh, "Can't fool a tracker."

Martin looked back and forth from Nick to Travis, and

back to Nick again, "I do not understand. *You* had the jewelry?"

"Not by my choice," Nick replied.

"It was planted on him," Travis said.

"Exactly," Nick replied. "The barmaid wasn't taking my purse when I caught her, she was putting it back."

Martin furrowed his brow, "I am not understanding this."

"Antoine drugged me, so she could pick my pocket without anyone in the place noticing her take my purse. He slipped the jewelry into my purse, left the tavern, with instructions for that wench to slip the purse back into my pocket. She didn't expect the drug to wear off the moment her hand was in my pocket. In her panic to escape, so as not to be arrested for a pickpocket, she had to tear me up to get away. She could always tell her employer that I was grabbing her, and she fought back, and ran from me."

"What would that accomplish?" Martin asked. "How would anyone know you had the jewelry?"

"You know what I think," Travis said to Nick.

"What is that?"

"I think, she was supposed to put the jewelry in your pocket, and then call the sheriff to check you. They would find the jewelry on you, and hang you for the crimes, letting Antoine and the gang escape, with the murderer hung, and they in the clear."

Nick nodded, "That's exactly right. The problem was, the drug wore off too fast, and by catching her picking my pocket, she would be arrested, not me. The plan was thwarted."

"But, now you had the jewelry," Travis remarked.

"I didn't know it at first, though," Nick said. "We were at the river boat, buying the knives. It was the first time I had opened that purse and actually looked in it since that day. I had just been throwing money in it, on top of the pouch with the jewelry. When I found it in my purse, I didn't know what to do. I couldn't let either of you see it. When we got to the outlaw's camp, and I saw the coins on the ground, I thought to throw the pouch down with them. By that, if it was found, it would not come back to me."

"It would have worked, except it went too far under the bush," Travis said. "I'm glad we cleared that up though. It had raised my suspicions about you."

Martin nodded, "It would have taken something to convince me you had not taken it. It is a good thing I did not know about it then."

"That's why I hid it, and then got rid of it. When I left the tavern," Nick continued, "I went home to clear my head from the drug. I threw my purse into a drawer and laid down. When I awoke an hour later, my head was clear, and I rode to St. Charles to see you, and bring your auction money. When I got there, I found the house burned. A man told me what had happened. I went to the hospital to see you, but you were unconscious. The doctor said you would be for a day, or so. I left, figuring to come back the next day.

"I began asking along the waterfront as to the gang, and learned they had tried to get on a boat, but there were none available. I realized that the only reason they wanted a boat was to escape into the wilderness to the west. I rode on, asking questions, and getting leads as to their travel. Because of his meeting to set me up, Antoine was behind them. I was closer to him than to the gang, and he was on foot, and I was mounted.

"I caught up to Antoine while he was walking down the road. On seeing me, he ran into the trees. I galloped after him, and caught him when he tripped and fell. I didn't say a word to him. I pulled him to his feet, and stuck my knife in his belly. I looked into his eyes, and said, 'You wretched filth, I told you to stay away from them.' Then, I ripped the knife up, and left him there in the woods, and rode on to Cote Sans Dessien. There, I learned of the horse thefts. I returned to St. Charles determined to get you in on the hunt."

"Yes, you talked me into pursuing the murderers with you," Martin said.

"I couldn't see you sitting and weeping when you could join me, and kill them."

"You were right, and I am glad you did."

"I never meant to deceive you, Martin. I was concerned, that if I told you I knew who they were, I would then have to explain why I knew them. If you knew all that, you would think I was an accomplice to the murders. Those men had to die for what they did, but it's Duncan Black I wanted the most, because he was the point of the sword that led the attack."

"How can you be sure he was?" Travis asked.

"Black was the one who showed up in my shop with Antione. The second in command of the gang often accompanied Antoine. That's how it was with me, when I was the second, and the man I killed, who was previous to me. That's how I knew he had made Black his second. Knowing Black's nature toward women, and his being the second, made him the obvious leader in the attack."

Travis nodded, "Yeah, I see that."

"It was confirmed tonight, when I overheard those two complaining about Antoine making Black his second instead of one of them, who had been with him the longest. Antoine had pulled Black ahead of them, and they didn't like it."

"Why do you think Antoine was so attached to Duncan Black?" Martin asked.

Nick hesitated a second, then replied, "Because, Duncan Black is Antoine's bastard son."

Martin stared at Nick for a moment, taken aback by the answer, then said, "That makes Black your cousin."

"Unfortunately, yes."

"Did your father know that?" Travis asked.

"I don't know. If he did, he never mentioned Duncan as his nephew."

"If Duncan is a bastard, then your parents might not

have acknowledged him," Travis said. "Many people do not acknowledge their relationship to such offspring."

"I learned of it by accident, myself," Nick said. "I overheard the two of them talking about it one night. I was surprised, to say the least. Later, I asked Antoine if it was true, and he said it was, but threatened to kill me if I told anyone in the gang. He had a common-law wife back east, a Scot woman, surname, Black. Duncan kept the mother's name, because being the true scoundrel he is, Antoine abandoned them."

"Why did it take so long for Antoine to bring him into the gang, if Duncan was his son?" Martin asked.

"Talking to Duncan later, he told me about his dirty work with Hudson Bay. That only added to the aversion I had for hm. He was one of their agents in charge of making trouble for the Metis, and driving out the Northwest Company. After the Battle at Seven Oaks, the law was looking for everyone involved. Duncan fled the Red River, and found the gang. Antoine took him in."

"We Metis fled because of the investigation," Martin said. "I did not expect they would investigate the Hudson's Bay men as well."

"Nothing came of the investigations," Nick said. "The whole matter of the battle was dropped when they learned the Hudson's Bay men started it."

Martin snorted, "That sounds about right."

"That explains the connection between Antoine and Black," Travis remarked.

"So, was Black an assassin hired to find me, or not?" Martin asked.

"After considering the situation, I'm sure he wasn't. Anything could have transpired in the years after I left the gang, but he was running from the British law. Knowing Hudson's Bay, I'm sure they washed their hands of him, along with everyone else in that Seven Oaks fight. He had been a Bay agent once, and obviously by what happened at the Hudson Bay camp, he is still connected enough to trade at a Hudson's Bay fort, but as far as being a hired assassin, no. His meeting you was as by chance, as much as their finding me again."

"Something put them in enough panic to head for the wilderness, after what happened at Martin's house," Travis broke in. "Otherwise, they would have just moved on. Something put them on the run."

"I believe I know what that is," Nick said. "Black, and the gang, was supposed to attack Martin, and rob him of the fur money, but Black being the slimy thing he is, took the women. That wasn't part of the plan. Antoine went there, and found they had molested a woman, and worse, two children. He grew angry over what had been done, knowing the law would never stop hunting them, and hang them when caught. He killed Colette and the girls, so they couldn't talk, set the house on fire hoping to cover the crimes, and sent them all west to hide. He took the jewelry, and held back to set me up for the crimes."

"That could well be," Travis said. "Antoine might have

just wanted to rob Martin, and Black ignored the plan, and took matters into his own hands. That destroyed all future crime prospects."

"Black would do that," Nick agreed. "While I was there, he was one to do what he wanted, and ignore the plan. Antoine took him to task for it, but did nothing more. This time, he went too far, and it was their undoing."

"It would also explain why Black partnered with Monk, and not a gang member, on the Sweetwater," Travis said. "They blamed him for their problems. He split the pelts with the gang, so they wouldn't kill him. They left him, and went their own ways."

"That's possible," Nick agreed. "They didn't like him, but being the animals they are, they followed him at Martin's house. They blamed Black, but they were willing participants in the crimes."

Martin sat silent, the images, and remembrances, too clear in his mind.

Nick looked at Martin, "I'm sorry, Martin, to bring up such painful talk."

Martin stared out at the stream, "Yes, it is very painful, however, I am glad we cleared this up." He turned his head to look at Nick, "Thank you for being honest about this. It is better knowing, than living with questions and speculation."

"Now, you know my story," Nick said. "Do you still want to ride with me? If you don't, I will go on alone, I'm not done hunting Duncan Black."

"Why shouldn't we want to ride with you?" Travis asked. "We started out on a mission together, and it's not finished."

"You are still my friend," Martin said. "I appreciate your openness, and your attempts to protect my family, and me."

Nick looked at both of them, "Then, in the morning we ride after Duncan Black."

"And, Luther Monk," Travis added.

"Finish this once and for all," Martin said.

2

At sunrise the three were up in the camp. Those who had their fill of rendezvous revelry, were also stirring about. Some were leaving the valley, others setting up coffee, and planning on an easy day. The worst of the men continued their drunken carousing, evidenced by the camps that had yet to rise, the men sleeping off the cheap whiskey. They would wake up with skull splitting headaches, and spend the day recuperating so they could go back at it again that night. Even Coon Eyes Charlie, and Hugo, had wasted all they were going to on celebration.

Travis was already riding for the camp of the dead outlaws. He was thinking about all Nick had told them the night before. He had suspected there was a violent history behind the man, and from all he had heard about river pirates, they were a vicious lot. It was to Nick's credit that he was man enough to break away, and man enough to tell them the truth. He understood why he had kept the secret this long. It surely would have tainted his feelings toward him, but now, Nick had proven his mettle and honesty, and he wanted him in their party.

The scavenger birds had not wasted any time in finding the bodies. They were flocking in the trees, and on the ground. A pack of coyotes trotted away as he approached. Two horses were still tied to the trees, their actions nervous, and wide-eyed, at the birds and coyotes. Two horses were missing, though, along with the packs of pelts, and packsaddles, that had been on the ground. Pulling the roan to a stop, he studied the area, scanning out, and around, looking for the two horses. They might have pulled loose, but he never knew horses to saddle and pack themselves.

It had been dark when they came on Nick, and his handywork, last night. It had just turned light when he left the camp an hour ago, headed here. There had been only a few hours in between. He dismissed the idea of Indians taking the horses and packs, this camp was too far removed from the Flathead and Nez Perce encampments, they wouldn't have known about it. No trapper knew what had happened out here, so that left only one answer, Monk and Black were here. The question was, were they watching when Nick killed the outlaws, then moved in, or had they come later to kill them, and take the pelts, only to find they were already dead? If it was them, they would add these horses and pelts to the others they had, bound for Fort Nez Perce. If it was someone else, they might have traded them off already. He'd swing by Jim's camp and ask him.

Bridger and Sublette were bundling pelts when Travis rode up.

Jim smiled at him, "Big Walker, yer up bright 'n early. Out for a mornin' ride, are yuh?"

"Sorta. Just to let you know, there's two men layin' dead, down the creek."

Jim closed one eye and looked at Travis, "Yuh know how it happened?"

"Yup. Did anyone bring you two pack loads of pelts this mornin'?"

Jim shook his head, "Nope. Some missin'?"

"Looks that way. Thieves stole from the thieves. Might be those outlaws we're after."

"Figger it to be Luther Monk?"

"Yeah, and Duncan Black."

"Headin' out to find 'em?"

"I'm sure they're out of here by now. Those Hudson Bay spies helped 'em get away, but we've got a good idea where to find 'em."

"Where's that?"

"Oregon Territory, Fort Nez Perce. They'll sell the stolen pelts there, and try to stay under the protection of the Hudson's Bay officials."

Jim nodded, "I know somethin' of that country. You might be interested in knowin', there's been talk among the men about payin' those Hudson's Bay fellers a visit this mornin', invitin' 'em to leave."

"Then, I should be in on that." Travis put his hand out to Jim, "Be seein' you around."

Jim shook his hand, "Watch yer topknot."

"Watch your'n." Travis reined the horse around. "By the way, there's two good horses down the creek. You might as well claim 'em before someone else does."

"I'll get 'em," Jim called back as Travis rode away.

Sublette came up to Jim, "Walker get those outlaws?"

"Appears so. Says they're down the creek. Two good horses to be claimed."

"Walker's like a mean dog, once he sinks his teeth into something, he don't let it go."

"That's Travis," Jim said. "We took in a lot of pelts; two more horses'll be good. I'm gonna git those before someone else does."

Travis returned to their camp. Martin was coaxing a fire to grow, and the men were in various stages of waking up. Martin looked up at him from where he knelt beside the fire, "You get the pelts to Bridger?"

"They were gone, horses, packs, pelts – gone."

Martin raised his eyebrows, "Did someone get them? Indians, another trapper?"

"It's only been a handful of hours. There wasn't time for the Indians to get 'em, and no trapper knew it was there."

Martin stood up, "Black and Monk? Maybe, they are still here."

"It had to be them, but I don't think they're here anymore."

Nick came out from the trees leading two horses he had taken to water. "What was that about Black and Monk?"

"The pelts, and two horses are gone," Travis replied.

"Someone beat you to them?" Nick asked. "If they did, they had to have known it was there."

"I stopped and asked Jim if anyone had come in this mornin' with the pelts," Travis said. "They hadn't. I think Black and Monk went to kill 'em, and take the pelts, but found 'em already dead."

Nick furrowed his brow in thought, "Possible. Either they saw me kill them, or intended to kill them and take the pelts. They weren't as gone as we thought."

"If you remember," Martin began, "we had considered the idea Monk and Black would ambush the other outlaws at the foot of the pass in Jackson's Hole, but they never showed up. We might have been right, just had the wrong location. They intended to kill them here, and take the pelts."

Travis nodded, "I think you hit it on the head. We had the right idea, but the wrong place."

"Doubling the pelts makes their trip to Fort Nez Perce more worthwhile," Martin said.

"I'm sure they're headed that way now," Travis said. "We need to get after them, but first, Jim told me that some of the men are goin' to the Bay camp to say goodbye. I'm headin' over there, wanna come?"

Nick grinned, "That sounds neighborly. It would be disrespectful of me not to attend."

"Throw some saddles on those horses, and let's go," Travis said.

"Several of the men jumped up. "Give us a minute, while we get our horses," Enoch called out. "I'm not too happy 'bout them helpin' those varmints git away after they murdered Billy."

"And, they tried to kill us," Jimmy added. "Anybody got some tar and feathers?"

Travis chuckled, "Sorry, Jimmy, fresh out."

Ten minutes later, the group was riding toward the Hudson's Bay camp. The closer they got to it, the more trappers they saw walking, or riding, in that direction. Word had spread quickly that the Hudson's Bay men had helped Monk escape his justice, and they would be held responsible for their actions. By the time they reached the camp they found it surrounded by at least fifty trappers who had friends murdered by Monk, and the outlaws he guided.

Looking over the heads of the trappers, Travis could see the four Bay men standing together, looking scared. Travis called out, "Hudson Bay!"

The Bay men, and most of the trappers, turned to look at Travis. "I told you to pack up, and get out. Since, you seem a little slow in your understandin', these men have come to help you on your way."

"What is the meaning of this?" demanded the Bay leader.

"The meanin' of this is, you helped two murderers escape, knowing who they were. Men who killed, and robbed, friends of these men gathered here. Those two were due for justice, to pay for their crimes, and you helped them escape. It's time for you to pack your camp, and go back to your own country."

"This *is* our country!" the leader shouted back. "*You* are the trespassers."

"Well, in that matter, you're in the right place to be buried on your own land then," Travis replied.

"Buried!" the leader shouted back. "You mean to kill us? That is preposterous, there are laws!"

"Hudson's Bay laws don't count for anything here," Nick shouted at him. "Your contrived laws make criminals out of honest men, and set yourselves as Lord and Master over Rupert's Land, and the people who live there. Now, you are trying to do it to this part of the country, and we don't like it. You enact punishment on men in your domain, we do the same in ours."

The trappers gave an affirming hurrah to Nick's speech. Then, moved in on the Bay men."

"Wait! Wait!" the leader shouted in a high-pitched, strained, and frightened voice. "We will leave. Give us time to pack our things."

The trappers stopped moving, and looked at them. Then, to Travis, to see if he had anything else to say.

"Five minutes," Travis said. "Be on your way, in five minutes."

The Bay men quickly scrambled to pack their camp gear. Several trappers led the Bay men's horses to their camp through the ranks of the men surrounding them. They dropped the lead ropes, then watched the Bay men as they picked up the ropes.

"Your five minutes is about up," Travis called out to the Bay men. "Best hurry up, these boys are gettin' anxious. I can't hold 'em back forever."

Several of the trappers looked at Travis and laughed. He wasn't holding them back, and they all knew it, but it sounded good.

Saddles were hurriedly thrown on the horses, cinches pulled, and bridles shoved in the horses' mouths. Two of the trappers saddled their pack horse, and tied the Bay men's pack on it. Handing the lead rope to one of the Bay men, the trapper said, "Thar, you ain't got no reason to linger about."

The Bay men mounted. The leader cast an evil eye on Travis, and shouted, "You will pay for this."

Travis met his eyes, "You don't want to meet again. It won't go well for you if we do. Now, get."

The group parted to let them ride out. They watched as the four Bay men struck the Teton River and followed it west. Aaron Dix, who was sitting on his horse beside

Travis, laughed, placing his palms together, finger tips pointed at the Bay men's exit, he moved them apart, "It was like Moses parting the Red Sea."

"It would have been more like what happened to the Egyptians once Moses passed through, if they didn't leave when they did," Travis remarked.

Aaron grinned, "Good thing they got their chariots going before the sea closed back in."

The group began to break up, heading back for their camps. Nick looked at Martin, who was beside him, and then Travis, "We had better pack up and get on Black's trail. They have enough lead on us."

Travis nodded, "Yeah, we need to get goin'."

"Are we going to ride directly to Fort Nez Perce, or try and track them?" Martin asked.

"We can't track 'em, there's been too many horses over this area," Travis replied. "Our best bet is to head directly for the fort, but I don't know that country. I want to talk to John Tyler, ask him about it."

They rode to Tyler's camp where the men of his party had watched the trappers surround the Bay men. They were standing, looking at Travis, Martin, and Nick as they came toward them. "Looks like you sent them on their way," Tyler called out.

"They decided it was safer back in Hudson's Bay country, than here," Travis called back.

"Come in and sit," Tyler invited.

"We need to get on our way," Travis replied. "We have to

catch up to the outlaws. We do need some help from you, though."

"Certainly, what do you need?"

"We're sure they're headed for Fort Nez Perce. Is following the Snake all the way there, best, or is there a way, cross-country, to get there faster?"

"You might be told of a route to the west, that requires crossing the mountains. There is a trail and pass that the Salish and Nez Perce use over it. We have used it, but it must be crossed in summer, for the snows come as early as September."

"This is mid-summer," Travis said. "Will it cut off days?"

"No, it takes the same days whether you follow the Snake River, or go over this pass," Tyler replied. "I would advise you to follow the Snake route. It is easier on the horses, and there is game along the way. The mountains have no game in them. There are bones of dead horses on that trail. You lose your horses up there, and you will die in those mountains."

Travis frowned, but nodded his acceptance of the answer. "I was hopin' we could go straight across, but the Snake trail does sound better. How far is it before the Teton River reaches the Snake?"

Tyler narrowed his eyes at Travis, "How familiar are you with the country west of here?"

"This is as far west as I've gone."

"The Teton River does not flow into the Snake," Tyler

said. "It flows due west into the Henry's Fork, then Henry's Fork flows south into the Snake River."

Travis sat on his horse, a perplexed look on his face. I was led to believe the Teton went to the Snake."

Tyler shook his head, "You were told wrong. Follow the Teton to Henry's Fork, then south to the Snake."

"I've only been up the Snake a short way, and that was on the south side. I guess Henry's Fork empties into the Snake further to the west than I've gone."

Tyler nodded, "Probably. The Snake takes a low horseshoe bend to the south of here, but where the Henry's Fork meets it, the Snake flows due west."

Travis nodded, "Thanks for gettin' me straightened out on that. I'd of been real confused. We'll follow Henry's Fork south to the Snake, then."

"That's right," Tyler said. "It's better that way."

"What is the Snake country like?" Nick asked.

"Flat," Tyler replied. "There are some rolling hills, but mostly the country lays out flat. That makes for easy traveling. There is water, grass for the horses, and as I said before, there is game. The only place you will climb any mountains will be the Blue Mountains, a couple days before the fort, however, there is a good trail over it. Then. it goes flat again once across, and stays like that to the Columbia River."

"Sounds like the way to go," Travis said.

"I must give you a warning, though," Tyler said.

Travis furrowed his brow, "What is that?"

"You just said it yourself, that is Hudson's Bay country, British held. It is not the states, or an American holding. You might be stopped at some point. Hudson's Bay, Governor Simpson, has ordered his officials to drive out, or arrest, everyone, not employed by Hudson's Bay, or carrying their license. If you are arrested, you will be taken to Fort Vancouver to be put on trial for any charges they want to press on you. You have also made enemies of those Bay agents. Should you encounter them in their territory, they will most certainly arrest you for their humiliation."

Nick ran his hand over his bearded jaw, "John is right. If we enter that fort, and we are not carrying Hudson's Bay licenses, we will either be ordered out of the territory, or, if the Bay agents we made enemies with, are there, we will be arrested. Traveling through the Oregon Territory, we will have to be on the alert for Hudson's Bay officials, just as much as we were for the Blackfeet."

Travis was looking at Nick, listening to what he said. He shook his head, "I almost made another mistake. I'm so used to goin' wherever I please, with only Indians to watch out for, that I didn't think about how much the British want to keep us out of the Oregon Territory."

"Are we still going to pursue them?" Martin asked.

"We are," Travis replied. "We just have to be cautious, and avoid the Bay officials."

"What about Luther Monk? He is not British, will they let him go through?" Martin asked.

Travis looked at Tyler, "What about that?"

"If Duncan Black wants to keep him as a partner, the Bay will give him a license," Tyler replied.

"But, they can't rob and murder trappers in the Oregon Territory," Nick broke in. "Every trapper in there works for Hudson's Bay. If they murder and rob Hudson's Bay employees, they will be hung. Black would know that."

"That leaves only two choices for Black," Travis said. "They have to come back to the American side to rob and kill, or stay in there, and not rob anyone. I can't see Monk goin' along with that idea, though."

"There is a third choice," Nick said. "Black could kill Monk, or have him jailed. Get him out of the way completely."

Travis held his eyes on Nick, "Sure. Once he's used Monk for all he's worth, why keep him. The trappers here have all sold their pelts, there's nothin' left to steal, and I doubt they'll want to hang around through the winter waitin' for more pelts. Knowing Monk, he will want to keep robbin' and killin' in the Oregon Territory."

"If Black wants to work for Hudson's Bay, he cannot have Monk with him doing that," Tyler said. "The Chief Factor in charge of the Oregon Territory, is John McLoughlin, at Fort Vancouver. He doesn't put up with law breakers. Bay employee, or trespasser, will feel his wrath if they are committing crimes."

"What would Black do, if he gets rid of Monk?" Martin asked Tyler.

"He will stay in the Oregon Territory, or go up to New

Caledonia, employed as a Hudson's Bay agent. That would be my guess," Tyler replied.

"Black was an enforcer for Hudson's Bay over the Red River Colony," Nick said to Tyler. "He was with the group that attacked the Metis at Seven Oaks. He enforced Hudson's Bay laws, and those of the Colony's governor. Does Hudson's Bay have enforcement patrols in the Oregon Territory?"

"Not actual patrols, however, any Hudson's Bay official, or agent, can stop anyone and question them. Since the Americans have been trying to come in there, they have been stricter on checking. That is how they catch American trappers, or anyone looking to settle, and run them out. The Hudson's Bay officials have arrest powers, should those they encounter resist the order to leave."

"In Rupert's Land, they arrest anyone they want to," Nick added.

Tyler nodded, "That's why me, and my companions, can never go back. We are now wanted men, and will be arrested should they catch us anywhere Hudson's Bay controls."

"Simply because, you did not sell your pelts to them?" Martin asked.

"Yes," Tyler replied. "That's all it takes to be in violation of Governor Simpson's laws. He believes that every pelt caught in their lands belongs to Hudson's Bay. Not to sell it back to them is considered theft. Many of his laws are not passed from England's House of Commons. He makes his own laws, own courts, own sentencing, with little over-sight from the House."

"England *did* tell Hudson's Bay to enforce the law, and create courts for trials," Martin remarked.

"They did," Tyler replied, "but they were supposed to enforce the House of Commons' approved laws, and proper trials, not create their own."

Nick looked from Martin, to Travis, "After listening to all this, I think, Black wants to be given a commission, and a post, but he won't get it if he runs with an American outlaw. Monk has become a burden, one he no longer needs, he will kill him."

"Black just needed Monk until he got to the Oregon Territory, where he would not be found for his crimes in the states," Martin said. "They robbed along the way, because that is what they do. Now, that he is where he wanted to escape to, he no longer needs Monk."

"There is more to the pelt thefts then habit," Nick said. "All those pelts will give Black the money to buy a post in the Hudson's Bay government. That's why they collected all they could along the way. He lost some in paying off the gang so they wouldn't kill him, but he planned on getting back from them all he could."

Travis nodded his agreement. "It's all starting to add up, but the gang splitting up did work to Blacks advantage. If he wanted a Bay post, he couldn't go into the Oregon Territory with a murderous gang. Now, he only needs to get rid of Monk, instead of all of them."

"Knowing, Black, he would use their anger against him to his advantage. He was clever that way," Nick agreed. "Like father, like son. Antoine would have done the same thing."

"How do you think we should do this, Travis?" Martin asked.

Travis sat in silence for a full minute before answering. "We will follow the Snake River, asking along the way of any Indian, or white man, we meet, about the men. Black's red beard will stand out as a curiosity among the Indians, they'll remember him, if they saw him. Then, hope for the best in finding them."

"One story at a time," Nick said.

"That seems to work pretty good," Travis replied.

Nick looked at Tyler, "What Indians will we come on?"

"It will be Nez Perce, and Shoshone country, most of the way. Once over the Blue Mountains it will be the Cayuse. They run the whole of the country north of the Malheur River, through the mountains, and onto the plains of the Umatallow River. They are a smaller tribe then the others, but they don't like white men. Hudson's Bay trappers wiping out the beaver, and game, have turned them sour on the white man. You meet them they'll likely attack, or at best, rob you and turn you around. They speak a tongue similar to the Nez Perce, who they sometimes align with, but not all the same, however, they do signs.

"At the Columbia River, will be the Wallawalla Indians. They are a big tribe, and control that whole area around the mouth of the Snake. They are friendly with the Cayuse, Palouse, and Nez Perce. They're not happy about Fort Nez Perce, and have made it hard on the Hudson's Bay men. They demand gifts, or they prevent all trapping and hunting, but they are not murderous like the Cayuse. Those are the Indians you will encounter where you're going."

"Alright," Travis said. "You've given us some good information to go on.

"What does Fort Nez Perce look like?" Nick asked Tyler.

"It was small, the palisades old, and falling in on some parts. The new Post Master is a Hudson's Bay officer named, McGillivray. He has been making improvements on the fort, and building up the walls, making the fort larger, and stronger. Inside are a powder magazine, store rooms, barracks, officer house, rooms of that nature."

"How many men hold it?" Nick asked.

"Seven, maybe, and the master."

"All I want from the fort, is to see if the stolen pelts are there, and learn where Black and Monk, went," Travis said. "Hopefully, we can get that information without gettin' into trouble." He turned to Tyler, "Thank you for the information. Good luck to you and your friends."

"Hope you find your men," Tyler replied.

"If you're up toward the Yellowstone come winter, we keep winter camp where the river flows into the lake. You're welcome to join us."

"We'll keep that in mind. Good hunting," Tyler replied.

3

Everyone had returned to the camp when they rode back in.

"What did you learn from those men?" Enoch asked Travis.

"Mostly directions, and to watch out for Hudson's Bay officials," Travis replied. "We did come up with an interesting idea about Duncan Black, and Monk. Now that Black's back with his own, he'll kill Luther Monk, and get himself a post in the Hudson's Bay government."

Several of the men walked up to them as they dismounted. "Shor," Jimmy agreed. "He don't need Monk no more, so why pack him along?"

Travis nodded, "That's right. Problem is, if he kills Monk, then *I* can't kill him."

"I'd say that's sorta out of yer hands now," Charlie said.

Travis frowned, "Pretty much, yeah."

"You know, every trapper, and discovery party, has been kicked out of the Oregon Territory," Aaron said. "You might not ever find him. How long do you plan to keep looking for him?"

"Until we find him, or decide it's wasted effort," Travis replied.

"Or, they throw yuh out," Charlie said.

"It will be like finding a single, specific grain, in a sack of wheat," Aaron remarked.

"I don't expect it to be easy," Travis replied, "but you know what, Aaron?"

"What's that?"

"That specific grain *is* in that sack."

Aaron chuckled, "You're not wrong."

Travis looked around to see Martin and Nick going through their supplies to be packed. Travis walked up to them. "We really need to lighten our load for this trip, just take what we need on one pack horse."

Nick looked at him, "That's what we were just discussing. "Whether we find Black, or not, we'll be coming back here. We don't need to haul traps, and extra gear. We just need food, and a few other things, only what one horse can carry."

Jimmy and Nels walked up them. "We heard what you was sayin'" Nels said. "We can take yer traps, and truck, on one of yer horses, and keep it at our cabin. You kin pick it up thar when you come back."

"That would work out real good, thanks," Travis replied. "When are you headin' back to the Poudre?"

"Soon," Nels answered. "Even Jimmy's had enough of this foo-fer-ah nonsense. Ain't like it used to be, too many greenhorns tryin' to prove somethin'. I must be gettin' old, cuz I miss my quiet valley, ain't much fer all this noise no more."

Travis nodded, "Yeah, I got used to solitude, and this here's too much commotion. Lookin' forward to some quiet again."

"Well, you boys jist sort out yer goods thar, and pack what yer takin'," Nels said.

"We'll make packs of the things we're not taking," Nick said. "That will make it easier for you, Nels."

Nels stood looking at Nick for a moment, "Ain't none o' my business, but wasn't yer name Prisque? Now, they're callin' yuh, Nick."

Nick grinned at him, "Long story, Nels."

Nels nodded, "Fair 'nough. So, we call yuh, Nick, now?"

Nick held the grin, "Yup."

Within the hour, Travis, Martin, and Nick, holding the lead rope to the one packhorse, were mounted. Their friends stood looking at them. "We'll see yuh when you get back," Nels said.

Travis grinned, "You will for sure. We can't catch many beaver without our traps."

Enoch walked up to them. "Thanks for everythin' you

did for me. You saved my bacon fer sure, and got my pelts back so I ain't destitute now."

Travis laughed, "Well, we all make mistakes."

Enoch burst out laughing. Might be so, might be so. See you in winter camp, if not sooner."

"Figure to be there," Travis said.

Charlie looked at Martin, "You're one skookum feller, Martin. Mighty good man to have in the party. Know yer dealin' with a lot, but yuh figure to stay in the mountains, or head back for the cities?"

Martin shrugged, "Do not know what I will do, yet. Got a lot of thinking to do."

"Then, maybe we'll see yuh in winter camp," Charlie said.

Martin looked at him, "Maybe. Be careful, Charlie."

"Watch yer top knot." Charlie then looked Nick over, "You don't say much, but you'll do to take along."

Nick smiled, "Thanks, Charlie."

Charlie laughed, "Travis you'd best git him outta here 'fore he talks my arm off."

With a final wave to the camp, the three rode out.

Reaching the remains of the Hudson's Bay camp, they swung around it, and picked up the Teton River, following it west. The tracks of the departing Bay men's horses were fresh. "We can follow these tracks," Travis said, as he leaned out looking at the horseshoe prints. I'm sure they're goin' right on top of Black's tracks."

"Sounds like, Fort Nez Perce is the only Hudson's Bay

fort this side of Fort Vancouver," Nick said. "We should find them there."

"Black has to sell his pelts, and the others will be anxious to report us to those in charge," Martin added.

"Right on both counts," Nick replied. "Those men in the camp were just agents, like Black was, they're not government officials. They'll want to tell their superiors how badly they were treated by the Americans. Kick us out, if we show up."

"I'm sure they told Black we were after him," Travis said. "I doubt he knew it before his visit to them. Now, he'll be watchin' for us, and gettin' out of sight."

They rode on through the day, the trail the Bay men left, stopped, and started, as they took breaks wherever shade trees were found. The land ran flat, the grass turned brown by the summer sun that pounded down from a flawless blue sky. There were few trees to offer respite from the heat, even along the river, the growth was mostly brush and willow. They had yet to reach Henry's Fork when the sun began to set, and they stopped to camp in the shade of a few riverside trees.

"They don't believe in trees out here, do they?" Nick remarked as he took off his hat, and wiped the sweat from his brow."

Travis wiped his sleeve across his brow, "Pretty hot country, that's for sure."

Dismounting, they unsaddled the horses, then took them to the water. Travis looked around, the grass was long enough for the horses, but was brown and bent from the heat. "We'll stake 'em out to graze. We're still in Nez Perce country, I don't expect them to steal our horses, so I don't think we need a night guard."

"I would feel better tying them to the trees during the night," Martin said. "Maybe, the Indians will not take them, but they could pull the stakes loose and run off. Being stuck in this hot, flat country without horses would be very bad."

"I didn't mean to stake 'em out all night," Travis replied. "We'll tie 'em to the trees, but one of us doesn't have to guard all night."

Martin nodded.

Martin opened the pack, and pulled out the coffee pot and frying pan. "Coffee and bannock," he said.

Nick was looking at the stream, "There's fish jumping in there. I've got fishing line and hooks, hold on for some fish."

Nick cut a long, willow sapling, then trimmed the twigs from it. Digging into his bag, he brought out a spool of line, and a little box with hooks.

"I'll stake the horses," Travis said to Nick, "you catch some trout."

Nick grinned, "That's the kind of work I like." He tied a length of line to the willow pole, then a hook to the line. Grasshoppers were plentiful, he caught one, and put it on the hook. Dropping the hooked hopper on the water's surface, it was instantly grabbed by a trout.

By the time Travis finished staking the horses, Nick had six big trout lying on the bank.

Travis looked at the fish, "I'd say that's plenty for tonight."

Nicked spun the line around the pole, "I think I'll keep this for the next camp."

Travis grinned, "I'm not staking horses every night while you fish."

Nick laughed, "If you're nice to me, I'll let you use my pole, and you can fish while I stake the horses next time."

Travis looked at him, "But, I have to be nice to you, huh? That's the catch?"

Nick nodded, "Yes."

Travis feigned like he was considering the deal. He glanced at the fish, then at the pole, then at Nick. He nodded slowly, "Okay, I suppose I can do that."

THE NEXT MORNING, they continued westward. After an hour, they could see the north-south line of trees in the distance that marked the course of Henry's Fork. The flat land was deceptive for distances, things looked closer than they actually were. It took another hour before they could see the shimmer of the water. A quarter-mile to their right, was a large herd of deer.

Travis pointed at the deer, "Fish is okay, but I prefer deer meat. Tyler said, there was game, but I don't know when we might see any again. Go on ahead, and wait for me at the river. Water the horses, while I get a deer, and we'll eat it tonight when we camp."

Martin and Nick rode on, while Travis parted from them. Fifty yards from the trees, a trapper, clad in dirty buckskins, rushed out toward them. They both stopped, and watched him run at a stumbling gait, closing the yards between them.

"What do you make of that?" Nick asked.

"He looks desperate. He might need help," Martin replied.

The trapper was breathing hard from his run, as he came to a stop in front of them. "I was hopin' someone would come by," the man wheezed. "I'm in a bad way, and need some help."

"What happened?" Martin asked him.

"I was set on by Indians," the trapper began. "They took my horse, my packhorse with all my food and supplies. They took my rifle, knife, even my possibles pouch – everything, then left me stranded here. I ain't had food in two days."

Nick furrowed his brow at the man, what he was saying didn't ring true. Travis had said they were in Nez Perce country, and they didn't attack trappers like he was saying. Besides, it wasn't that far to walk back to Pierre's Hole, where there was plenty of help. Why be stranded here starving for two days?

The trapper looked from Nick to Martin, his eyes pleading for help.

Nick tipped his head to the east, "Why didn't you just walk back to Pierre's Hole? Rendezvous is still on."

"That's a long way to walk in this heat, and I was weak from hunger," the trapper replied.

"Walk at night, then," Nick said. He was suspicious of the man's story. Two days without food shouldn't stop a mountain man, unless he was a greenhorn, and this man didn't look like a greenhorn.

"If you could just give me some food, I could probably make it back there."

Nick glanced at Martin, who was frowning at the man, "Are you believing this?"

Martin shook his head, "No." He looked at the man, "What are you really doing out here?"

At that, the man reached up, grabbed Martin's arm, and yanked him off the horse. As Martin hit the ground, the trapper grabbed the reins, and tried to mount the horse.

Nick kicked his horse at the man, smashing him between the two horses. He let out a grunt and fell to the ground. Getting to his hands and knees, he crawled under the horse's belly, but Martin grabbed his foot and yanked him back. The trapper kicked his hand away, and got to his feet. He tried to mount from the right side, but the excited horse was moving too much for him to toe the stirrup. He looked behind him, then took off sprinting across the ground, heading for the riverside trees.

Travis bolted past Nick and Martin. The big roan caught up to the fleeing man as he reached the river, and rammed into him. The man somersaulted twice, landing in the river, then flaying water, he attempted to get on his feet and make his escape across the river.

Travis pushed the roan into the river, latched his big hand around the back of the man's buckskin shirt, and dragged him back onto the shore. Throwing him to the ground, he jumped off the horse, and grabbed the man as he struggled to get away. Punching him in the face, the man landed on his back, gasping for air, blood trickling from his nose.

Nick and Martin galloped up to them, pulling the horses to a sliding stop. "Who is that?" Nick asked.

Travis glowered down at the gasping man, "*That*, is Luther Monk."

"We knew there was something wrong with his story," Nick said.

"He was telling us how he was stranded, and needed help, but he was only trying to divert our attention to steal a horse," Martin said.

"He's a slimy, lyin' weasel," Travis said. "Why was he stranded?"

"He said he was attacked by Indians, and they stole everything he had. He was hungry, and wanted food so he would have the strength to walk back to Pierre's Hole," Martin replied.

Travis snorted, "He got deserted is more like it."

Monk's shocked mind began to clear as he looked up at Travis' fierce, glaring eyes. He tried to crawl backwards from him, his face reflecting fear. Travis stood on Monk's foot causing him to cry out in pain.

"What happened to Duncan Black?" Travis asked him.

Monk's eyes widened in surprise that Travis knew about Black.

"Yeah, we know about him," Travis said to him. He gestured toward Martin, "Black, and his gang, murdered that man's family, those two have been on his trail ever since St. Charles. I joined the hunt at Fort Osage, when I saw you were with them."

Monk's wild eyes flickered rapidly across all of them, "I had nothin' to do with what they did."

"No, but you had plenty to do with killin' Frenchie Marier. Then, you murdered Warren Gentry, and Kelly, because they saw you do it. Then, you tried to kill Jimmy and Nels because they knew, too. Only thing, they tripped up your game, and put you on the run. Then, you murdered Arthur Lakey, and his partner."

"I . . . I, never did that. Black, and his gang, did that. I . . . I tried to stop 'em," Monk stammered out.

"Liar," Travis said casually. "We've followed that gangs blood trail all the way to here, and you led 'em."

Monk pulled his foot out from under Travis' boot, and pushed himself backward across the ground, putting space between him and Travis, but too scared to get to his feet. "You got it all wrong, Walker. Okay, I admit, you caught me stealin' a beaver from your trap, and shot me. I'll give you that, but I never killed all those men."

"You were traveling with Duncan Black," Travis went on. "He's a Hudson's Bay man, did you know that? He just needed you, to get him to the Oregon Territory, to escape his crimes, and rejoin Hudson's Bay where he will be protected. Were you waitin' with him here, for the others to catch up? Waitin' with the stolen pelts, and when they showed up, Black and his Bay friends, turned on you. They took everything from you, and left you to die out here. Tell me how wrong I am?"

Monk licked his lips, as he starred up at Travis.

"Where's Black goin'?" Travis asked.

"Down the Snake, there's a Hudson's Bay fort there," Monk answered. "Him and me were goin' there to sell the pelts. Then, he was goin' to get me in with his friends there."

Travis snorted, "He's as big a liar as you are. You trusted him, and he stabbed you in the back."

"Yeah, you're right, Walker, that's what he did. They got here, and took everything from me," Monk began in a tone of self-pity. "Black said, he was done with me. They took the pelts, my horse, gun, knife, everything. Told me to find my way back, but if I went into their territory, they'd kill me."

"Well, Luther, you've had a run of luck, but it seems to have run out – right here," Travis said in a glacial tone. "Nick, get that rope I picked up."

Monk's eyes widened with terror, "What are you gonna do?"

"Murder is punishable by hangin', even out here," Travis said in the same tone. "I know of at least five you're responsible for, but we can only hang you once."

Monk scrambled backwards, his moccasins digging into the soft ground, pushing dirt and dead leaves out as he fought to escape. *"You can't do that! You can't do that!"* he cried, tears streaming down his face into his beard. "I get a trial. You have to take me back to St. Louis for a trial."

"Okay, we'll give you a trial. I declare this to be St. Louis," Travis said. "The court of St. Louis is now in session," he called out. "Judge Travis Walker presiding. We don't have twelve jurors, we only have two, so they'll each vote six times."

"You can't do that!" Monk sobbed

"Luther Monk," Travis said in an ominous tone, meant to imitate that of a judge. "You are charged with five counts of murder. How do you plead?"

"I didn't do nothin'!" Monk screamed.

"Jury, how do you find the defendant?"

Nick and Martin each repeated the word, 'guilty' six times.

"Luther Monk, the jury has found you guilty as charged. I sentence you to be hanged by the neck until you are dead."

Monk flipped over onto his hands and knees trying to crawl quickly away, but Travis grabbed him and slammed him face-down on the ground. Martin tied his hands behind his back with a leather thong. Nick made a loop in the rope and threw it over an extending tree branch.

Travis and Martin yanked Monk to his feet. Nick put the noose over his head, and tightened it around his neck. Monk was screaming and crying hysterically. With a steady pull on the rope, Nick stretched Monk's neck until he could only squeak. Above his beard his face turned red, as tears poured down his face.

The three pulled the rope until Monk's kicking feet were two feet off the ground. They tied the rope off to a sapling.

They gathered the reins to their horses, "Now, there's only one left," Travis remarked as he stepped into the saddle. The three rode away from the scene.

4

They rode out the day with little conversation. Hanging a man was a sobering experience. It was one thing to shoot a man in a fight, even executing the gang murderers like they did, was one shot, and leave the body. It was another to put a rope around a man's neck, and hang him from a tree while he kicked and choked.

Luther Monk was a vicious murderer with no conscience, or morality to him, he had earned the justice due him. Had he been tried for five counts of murder in St. Louis, he would surely have been hanged. The pirates, for murders and rape, especially of children, would have been hung by a mob before the law could hang them. The Rocky Mountain court was the only one they had to deal with the likes of Luther Monk, and the cutthroat gang. It had spoken, yet it was not something to gloat on, justice served was its own entity. Once served, it was best to move on.

It was a half-day ride from the mouth of the Teton River, to the mouth of Henry's Fork. At the confluence, Henry's Fork, and the Snake came together in a V, the darker, cold water of Henry's Fork melded into the lighter-colored, warmer water of the Snake. The two waters formed a dark and light division until the Snake took control of the flow, merging it all into the same light color.

Both banks were shaded with tall elm and cottonwood trees. Hackberry trees, and a few pines, were surrounded by low-growing brush. Robins had gathered in the trees singing their melodic warbles, crows in the higher branches squawked in their raspy tongue, and blackbirds, their wings flashing red as they flited through the riverside brush.

Travis stopped and looked up and down the Snake. Martin and Nick pulled up beside him. "So, this is the Snake River I've been hearing about," Nick remarked. "Guess we're on the right track."

Travis looked downstream, "Good thing Tyler straightened me out about the rivers, or I would have thought Henry's Fork was the Snake, and when we got here, I'd be scratching my head wondering what this river was."

"It is all set right, now," Martin said. "I am ready for a break; this morning was an odd experience."

"It's a good spot for a rest," Travis agreed. He dismounted, and led his horse to a low spot on the river bank to drink."

Martin did the same. Nick led the pack horse into the shade of the trees. Travis had not made it to the herd of deer before he saw Monk pull Martin from the horse, and rushed back, but he shot a deer along the way, and tied it to the top of the pack. Nick pulled the deer off, and then the pack and saddle. He unsaddled his horse, and led both horses back to the river to drink. Travis and Martin unsaddled their horses, and staked them in the shaded grass. Travis took the pack horse from Nick, together they staked the horses out with the other two.

Taking a length of leather-braided rope, Travis hung the deer from a tree branch by a back leg. Skinning down part of the hide, he cut out pieces from the hindquarters. By the time he had collected enough meat for their meal, Martin had gotten a small flame to ignite a pyre of dry twigs.

After several minutes of adding bigger sticks, the fire rose to a workable level. Nick put the ready coffee pot beside the flames.

Travis cut sticks to hang the meat pieces on. Then, skewering the meat on them, he hung the meat over the flames, anchoring the stick ends down with rocks. He stood up straight and made a slow scan around them. He began to walk away, eyes searching the ground.

"What are you looking for?" Nick asked him.

"If this is a good place for us to camp, then the Bay men, camped here as well. I was hoping to find their campsite, and get an idea if Black is with them, or if they left anything behind."

"I'll help you," Nick said. He stood up and began searching in the direction opposite Travis.

Martin watched them from his place at the fire. The meat began to spit and sizzle, he rolled the sticks to cook the top sides of the meat. After the coffee had boiled for a few minutes, he removed it to from the flames. His mind was filled with images of Monk screaming for his life, overlaid with imagined visions of his beloved wife and daughters screaming for their lives. Tears began to roll down his cheeks, being lost in his beard. He wiped them away with his fingers.

He had not known Luther Monk, but he was cut from the same material as Duncan Black, and his gang of scum, and that material was to found at the bottom of an outhouse hole. Monk got exactly what he deserved. It was a bit unnerving to feel the weight at the end of the rope, and his thrashing about, yet it was by his own doing. He thought it would be a fine justice to see Black crying for mercy, and then the feel of pulling him up. He wanted to hang Duncan Black; it was better than giving him a quick death by a lead ball.

"I found it," Travis called out to Nick.

Nick turned and walked back to where Travis stood.

Travis walked along a line of horse tracks, pointing to them, "Ten horses picketed on a line from here to here. Five saddle horses, and five pack horses. Which means Black is with them, and him and Monk, did take the horses and pelts from the outlaws you killed, because they only had two pack horses before then."

"They knew where the other gang members were, and planned to kill them for the pelts. I just beat them to the killing part," Nick said.

"They hadn't left after meeting with the Bay agents, like I thought," Travis remarked.

"No, they had more killing in mind, and retrieving the pelts they gave in the split."

"Ten horses will create a sight, anyone who saw them will remember. They'll be together now until Fort Nez Perce."

"That will make separating Black from them a lot harder," Nick said with a scowl.

"We'll just have to figure out a way to get him."

"We don't want to kill the Bay agents," Nick said. "That would go very bad for us."

Travis shook his head, "No, we don't want to do that, not unless it's self-defense."

"What do you think they did with Monk's horse?"

"Turned it loose somewhere between here and there, so he couldn't get it back," Travis replied. He resumed his search of the area. Finding the remains of their campfire, he sifted through the charred pieces of wood, and the ash. "It's plenty cold."

Nick watched him, "That would put them a day or two ahead."

Travis felt something hard in the ash. He picked up some solid items, burned black and coated in ash. He blew them clean, and looked at them. He sifted some more, and found metal pieces, and lead balls misshapen from the heat.

"What do you have there?" Nick asked.

"They burned Monk's possibles pouch. Here's a metal striker, and a piece of flint. Lead balls, and a small knife blade with the handle burned off."

"You think they would have just thrown it away, why bother to haul it along and burn it?" Nick asked.

Travis shrugged, "Keep him from gettin' it back if he followed them, I guess. They probably kept his rifle and knife. They wanted him to die out here, but not kill him for some reason. I have no idea why they didn't just kill him."

Nick stared at the pieces in Travis' hand for a moment, then said, "I do. Black, and the Bay agents, know you're after him, and Monk. When the Bay agents joined him at the river, they decided to leave Monk behind so you would catch him, and give them time to get ahead. They might have hoped, if you got Monk, you'd stop there, and go back."

Travis nodded his understanding, "And, leave Black in

the clear. They threw Monk to the wolves, hoping to satisfy the wolves."

"Yes. Black learned that from Antoine. When pursued by the law, or vigilantes, pick the man you have the least use for, and feed him to them. The hope is, they will be satisfied with his blood, and leave the others go. You told the Bay agents that Black and Monk were wanted for murders, but not the murders in St. Charles, right?"

"That's right. I never mentioned the St. Charles murders."

"So, they know nothing about Martin, or his family. Black would never tell them about that. He has no idea Martin is with you, and unless he saw me kill those outlaws, he doesn't know about me either. As far as the Bay agents are concerned, you wanted Black and Monk for the trapper murders. So, they gave you, Monk. They have no idea Martin and I are after Black for Martin's family."

"You're right. They think that I'm the only one following them for the trapper murders and robberies. Black convinced them to throw me Monk, that would satisfy my hunt. I would kill him, and Black was free to go on."

Nick nodded, "Monk had no idea who Martin and I were. He saw us, and thought to take one of our horses, and escape you. We have the element of surprise against Black, he doesn't know we're still after him."

"He thinks he's in the clear, and not watching his backtrail."

"That's right. Even if Black sees you, he won't know who you are. As for me, he won't recognize me from a distance. He wouldn't know who to watch for, even if he did watch."

"As flat as this land is, it should be easy to spot five riders and five loaded pack horses, even at a distance," Travis said. "If we can get close enough, we can see where they go."

"Come on back to the camp, I have something that will help," Nick said. He began walking to the camp. Travis followed him wondering what he had.

"What did you find over there in the fire?" Martin asked.

"They burned Monks possibles pouch. There were some things in the ashes," Travis replied. "We put together that Black, and the Bay agents, think, only I'm following them for the trapper murders, they don't know about you and Nick. Black fed Monk to me, thinking I would kill him, leaving them to go on in the clear."

Martin considered the idea, then agreed, "You are right, there is no reason Black would know Nick and I are after him. You told the Bay men about the murders, but we were not with you. That puts us at a good advantage, if Black does not know we follow him."

"That's what we were thinkin'," Travis said.

Nick dug into his bag in the pack, and came out with a narrow wooden box. Travis looked at him, and the box. "What's that?"

Nick opened the box, and took out a brass tube, and set the box down.

"Is that a spyglass?" Travis asked with a hint of excitement rising in his voice.

Nick removed the cap from the objective lens, and pulled the telescoping instrument out to its full fifteen-inch length. He grinned at Travis, "Yes, it is." He handed it to him. "It's all brass, but I dulled it down, you don't want it reflecting in the sun when you're watching someone, or something."

Travis grinned, "Like a cargo boat?"

"Maybe."

Travis put it up to his eye and looked around, "Oh, this will be helpful. I can see all the way to the far bend of the river."

"Might give us a chance to spot them from a distance," Nick said.

Martin stood up next to them, "Can I have a look?"

Travis handed the glass to him.

"You never brought this out before," Travis said to Nick.

Nick grinned, "You already suspected me, and if I brought out a pirate's spyglass?"

Travis laughed, "You could have said it was to spot beaver huts, or elk."

"And, you would have believed that," Nick said with a skeptical tone.

"No, but you could have said it."

Martin handed the glass back to Nick, "That is a nice glass."

"It's a seaman's glass, made in France," Nick said as he took it back. "It's a duplicate of the one Jean Lafitte carried in his pocket. So said, the Frenchman who I bought it from."

"And, you thought I would suspect you of bein' a pirate just because you had Jean Lafitte's spyglass?" Travis remarked with a laugh.

Nick laughed, but did not comment.

Travis pointed at the glass, "Maybe we'll get lucky, and spot 'em."

"They won't be in a hurry," Nick said as he closed the spyglass and put it back in the box. "They think they're safe, and the pack horses will slow them down. If we move faster, we might overtake them enough to see them through the glass."

OVER THE NEXT three days they followed the winding course of the Snake River. It was a wide, smooth-flowing waterway that curved, and split around, numerous islands. The weather remained hot, with shade to be found only where the tall trees grew along the river, yet there were miles where the river ran through treeless, barren land.

The shod tracks of the Bay's horses had been obliterated by the unshod tracks of Indian horses. It was on the third day, from the confluence of Henry's Fork, that a hunting party of Shoshone, moving to the east, appeared in the distance. There were a large number of men, women, pack horses, and travois devices in the group. All loaded with buffalo meat, and topped with buffalo hides. Ten men broke from the group and rode toward them.

Travis stopped the roan, "Shoshone, they're always friendly."

The Indians stopped in front of them, they were showing an interest in the Palouse stud. The hunt chief pointed at the roan, "Nez Perce war horse. You trade for him, or take in battle?"

"You speak English well," Travis said to him.

"I learn from white trappers," he pointed to the east, "over there."

"I traded for the Nez Perce horse," Travis said. "The Nez Perce, and the Shoshone, have always been my friends. I don't fight my friends."

The chief nodded his approval. "English mans, Hudson Bay, say they own this land, and want to keep trappers out. Are you trapping?"

Travis shook his head, "We are hunting a white man, a child and woman killer. He is with four English mans, and five pack horses. He is a man with a big red beard, have you seen them?"

"Two days back, they were here, when we pass going west to hunt."

Travis nodded, "That is about how far they are ahead of us."

"Who did red beard kill?"

Travis pointed at Martin, "His wife and daughters. There were a whole party of 'em that did it. We have been tracking them for a long time. We've killed all but the one with the red beard."

"We ask them where they are going," the chief went on. "They say, they are going to the Hudson Bay fort on the Snake River. I do not know of that fort."

"It's a long way from here. That's where we're headed," Travis said. "We figure to catch 'em there."

"There is such a fort?" the chief asked.

"From what I'm told," Travis replied. "We've never been there, but the Snake is a long river."

"I have never follow Snake River to the end." The chief pointed down the river, "Follow the river one day, then, there is long hole in the ground that the river runs through. There will be no water for three days. That is as far as I have follow the river. No reason to go that way again. No water, no buffalo, not even deer."

Travis looked down the river as the chief pointed, he nodded, "That doesn't sound good." He looked back at the chief, and pointed to the northwest, "You were hunting there?"

With a nod, the chief replied, "Yes. Watch out for English mans, they will tell you leave." He reined his horse around, and led his men back to the hunting party.

Travis looked at Martin and Nick, "We haven't gained anything on 'em, but we're on the right track. They have to follow the river to reach the fort. We'll just stay on it as well."

"That stretch with no water does not sound appealing," Martin remarked.

"No, it doesn't," Travis replied. "They have to go through it, too. Maybe, it'll slow 'em down."

"The next hill we come to, I might be able to spot them with the glass," Nick said.

"You might, they've got no reason to hurry," Travis replied.

BY THE END of the following day, they were encountering great piles of rock, and the river was narrowing toward a deepening ravine. Sagebrush was covering the ground in between the upheavals of rock formations. "I have never seen anything like this," Martin said. "I wonder if this is the hole the Indian was talking about?"

"Looks like a ravine, or canyon," Travis said. "The river does go into a long hole, like he said.

"If any country was going to be dry for three days, this ugly chunk of land would be it," Nick remarked. He pulled the spyglass from his saddlebag, pulled it open, put it to his eye, and looked down the river over the changing terrain. "Oh, my Lord," he whispered. "I'm glad we're on this side."

"What is it?" Travis asked.

Nick handed him the glass, "Take a look. That's the long hole, alright."

Travis put the glass to his eye. "Oh, that's a little scary, and it runs forever."

"Okay, my turn," Martin said.

Travis handed him the glass. Martin looked across the country, "Looks like the earth just cracked open. What is this?"

"It's a canyon," Travis said. "The deepest, longest canyon, I've ever seen."

"Will it end?" Martin asked.

"I hope so," Travis replied. "He said, three days. I can see that, but I hope he meant it was *just* three days."

Nick took the glass back and looked again. "The land on the top is fairly flat, but with great upheavals of rock. I don't think we'll be able to see them over this terrain, too many places to be out of sight." He took the glass down and held it.

"Well, we know that it goes to the Columbia River, and there's a fort on it, so it has to end," Travis said.

"It looks dry as a bone, as far as the glass can see up that way," Nick said. "He said there was no water for three days, that was as far as he went. I wonder if he meant, he went for three days without water, then turned back, or if it was three days before he saw water again?"

"It's hard to tell with Indians," Travis said. "Distance to them is in days, and they ain't specific on details. He could have meant it either way."

Travis looked around him at the changing landscape of rock, sage, and sparse grass. Then. To the river disappearing into an ever-deepening canyon. Dismounting, he unhooked his leather canteen from the saddle. "We have no idea how far that country actually goes. Better camp here for the night, water the horses good, and fill our canteens, it's goin' to be a while before we see water again."

5

Through the next day they stayed along the rim of the canyon. The further west they traveled the deeper the gorge grew until the walls of the canyon were sheer vertical stone, hundreds of feet deep. The Snake River was a mere ribbon of water at the bottom of the gorge. The terrain above the walls had returned to flat, arid land, except where wedges of stone had been forced above ground by some great upward thrust of the earth at one time.

The scorching July sun sapped the life from man and plant alike. Sagebrush dominated the landscape, yet even this arid-land plant was scattered, and many of the plants were dead, dry skeletons. A smattering of stunted juniper trees broke up the bleak landscape. There was little grass for the horses, what there was of it was brown, brittle, and had the appearance of stunted wheat. Water was as nonexistent as shade. The only thing in abundance were the rattlesnakes that lay in the shade of the rocks and sage plants.

The horses bore a permanent coating of white sweat that dried almost as fast as it appeared. Their steps were slow, their heads hung from the heat and lack of water. The men let the horses move slowly, not forcing them. Killing them would not get them closer to the men they sought.

Nick sat on his horse, his countenance drawn down by the heat, "What a God-forsaken land," he muttered. "Hot, no water, and more poisonous snakes then I ever knew existed. Why would Hudson's Bay fight so hard to keep something like this?"

"Probably why they never built a trading fort out on this end," Travis replied.

Nick snorted, "Yeah, nothing here to trade for."

"It's a big country, though. I'm sure there's plenty of nice parts that they want to horde."

"THIS CANNOT BE ALL of the Oregon Territory," Martin said. "They certainly are not creating a fur desert, as John Tyler described, to protect this. The further north you go, anywhere, the land gets greener and wetter."

They rode on with no more conversation, as it required too much effort to work up the energy for pointless talk.

Stopping for the night, Travis dismounted with a groan. Taking the canteen from his saddle, he shook it, a little was left in it. He had never needed one that held more than a couple cups of water, as water was plentiful in the Rockies. He hadn't expected to run into a desert like this. "How much water do each of you have left?"

Martin and Nick shook their canteens that were similar to Travis'. "A mouthful," Nick said.

"About the same," Martin replied.

"We need to give it to the horses," Travis said. "They've been sweatin' bad."

Staking the horses on the dry grass, they trickled the last of the water into their palms to let the horses suck it in. It wasn't much, but it was better than nothing. That night they ate dried deer meat, and some cold bannock from their saddlebags. Then, laid their blankets on the hot sand. They took turns through the night guarding the horses, and chasing off rattlesnakes that invaded their space. In this arid land of heat, no water, or food, losing the horses was a certain death sentence.

IT WAS mid-afternoon the next day, when Travis felt a bee buzz by his face. He stared after the little insect as it disappeared from sight making a direct flight to the northwest of their position. Then, a second buzzed past him. He stopped the roan, and searched the ground around him. He spotted several bees crawling on a low rock outcrop, as several more flew out of a crack and followed after the first two. Travis watched their flight, his eyes squinting against the glare of the sun.

"What is it?" Martin asked.

"Bees," Travis said.

Martin furrowed his brow, "Bees? There is nothing here for bees to feed on."

"No, but they have a hive under that rock right there. That means, they have a source of food, and more importantly, water, somewhere close." He pointed in the direction the bees had flown, "Several just buzzed in that direction."

Nick looked where Travis had pointed, "Maybe, there's water over there."

"It's a good chance there is," Travis said, as he moved the roan to the northwest in the direction the bees had gone."

Rock outcroppings, and walls of rock, extending out from the canyon wall once again dominated the terrain. Ahead of them, rock rose up, forming a fortress-like barrier that they saw no way of penetrating, yet the bees had gone this way. The closer they drew to the edge of this new canyon, the more animal tracks they spotted going toward it.

"Everything's goin' this way," Travis said. "There has to be water in there."

Nick stopped, and pulled out his spyglass. Studying the

rock canyon for a full minute, he lowered the glass. "I don't see any opening."

"There has to be a trail through it, or the animals wouldn't be headed that way," Travis said.

Lines of animal tracks were converging into a single trail, that descended down through a ten-foot-wide break in the rock fortress. The horses suddenly jerked their heads up, their nostrils flared open, and their pace quickened. "They smell water," Travis said. "Give them their heads, they'll lead us to it."

Descending into the canyon was a trail, enveloped by a corridor of high stone walls. As they went on, it began to widen, until an open swath filled with tall sage, and green vegetation, led the way to the sparkling gem of a small lake tucked into an enclosure of stone. The horses' paced picked up excitedly as they made their way toward the water. They had to pull back on the reins to keep the horses from running over the rocky, uneven ground, in their rush for water. They didn't need a horse to break a leg.

Reaching the water's edge, there was only a small, level opening where the horses could reach the water, the rest of the lake was surrounded by rugged rock. Dismounting, they held onto the reins letting the horses put their muzzles into the water and suck it in. The pack horse, blocked back by the three other horses, was becoming frantic trying to push past them to the water.

"Don't let 'em drink too much, too quick," Travis said.

"They'll get sick. Pull their heads up, they can drink again later. Get the packhorse in here."

They had to fight the horses to pull their heads out of the water, but they did, and moved them back from the edge. The three horses stood, water dripping from their muzzles, as Nick moved the excited pack horse to the water. The horse stabbed his muzzle in and drank. Nick gave him a few seconds, then pulled his head out. The horse resisted him, but Nick led him back to where the others stood.

One at a time, the men went on their knees to the water, while the other two held the horses. "Oh, that is cold water," Martin said. "Sweet, and cold."

Martin took the horses from Nick to let him drink.

When they had all drank, they let the horses have another short drink. Taking the horses back to the grass on the trail, they had to tie them to the sage plants, as the ground was too rocky to drive in the stakes.

The men sat in the shade of the canyon walls, a cool breeze drifting off the water. "We'll stay here tonight, and move on in the morning," Travis said.

"I like that idea," Martin remarked. "These have been foul days, that I never anticipated."

"I wonder how much more of this nasty, rock strewn plain, we have to go through?" Nick asked.

"Until we're out of it," Travis replied. "The Shoshone said three days."

"I hope he was right," Nick said. "I wonder how those

Bay agents, and Black, are handling this. I'm sure they didn't have your skill in finding this water. Black liked his easy pleasures; he was never one to rough it. He liked taverns, meals, drink, and comfort."

"There's no other horse tracks," Travis said. "They never came down here."

"I do not think he found any of those pleasures, anywhere, after leaving St. Louis," Martin remarked.

"When we catch him, we'll be sure and ask him how he liked it," Travis said with a laugh. He looked up the way they had come, several deer were walking down the trail. "How about some fresh meat," he said as he picked up his rifle.

IT WAS late afternoon of the following day when, to their delight, the canyon walls steadily decreased like stairsteps going down. The river widened out over the valley as it opened again. Trees, and plant growth, showed profusely along the river bank, and spread inland with green grass, and plenty of room to ride alongside the river. There was shade under the trees. The day was hot, but a breeze blowing across the river valley stirred the heated air.

"Oh, this is nice!" Nick proclaimed, as they dropped down into the valley.

"He said, three days, and that's how long it was," Travis said. "I'm glad he meant it that way. Another couple of days of that, and I'd be questioning my good sense about being out here, or goin' mad."

"Tyler said it was good water and grass all the way," Martin remarked. "He must have come through in the spring, or he forgot about the canyon."

"Probably both," Travis replied. "Information is passed on, but it's not always accurate, or complete." He studied the river, and hills above them, as they rode down to the river.

Reaching the water, they let the horses drink. Then, they drank. The water was not as cold and sweet at the spring-fed lake the past day, but it was water.

Travis stood up from taking a drink, and filling his canteen. Pushing the cork back into the top, he said, "How far ahead they are now is anyone's guess."

"The best we can do is keep going to the fort, and see," Martin said.

"We just have to make sure we don't get thrown out of the country, or arrested, before we find 'em." Travis said.

"We'll think of something when we get there," Nick said. "The dice might roll in our favor."

Travis nodded, "Life does have a way of changin' things very quickly. I believe that's something we're all familiar with here."

Martin and Nick nodded their agreement.

"I think the best thing to do right now is to rest the horses for a day, and then keep goin' to the Columbia," Travis said. "See, what we see."

"We have come this far, and through the last agonizing three days, I do not want to stop now," Martin said.

"No, we're not stoppin'," Travis said. "We'll make our plan when we get there."

The rest of the day was spent resting in the shade of the riverside trees. The horses were staked on the grass, and moved every couple of hours to graze new spots. Come dark, they tied the horses to the trees around the campsite. The next day was spent in rest as well. They anticipated more hard country ahead, and wanted to go into it with rested horses, and themselves, refreshed.

AFTER TWO DAYS OF REST, the step of the horses was quickened. The three scanned the country as they rode, searching for dangers. "I wonder why we have not seen any Indians," Martin remarked.

"If we are still in Shoshone country, they might have packed up and headed for the mountains to escape the summer heat," Travis said. "That huntin' party we met, back behind us, likely had their village set up on Henry's Fork."

Martin nodded, "That makes sense. Except for right along the river, this is an inhospitable country for them to live."

"You notice something else," Nick broke in.

"What is that?" Martin asked.

"What Tyler said about that Simpson having Hudson's Bay killing all the beaver to keep the Americans out, how much fresh beaver sign do you see?"

"None," Travis replied. "A lot of old beaver cuttings, but nothing fresh. They did a good job of wiping out the beaver alright."

The day was waning into late afternoon when they spotted campfire smoke drifting out of the riverside cottonwoods. "Whether it's Indians, or trappers, it's the first humans we've seen since the Shoshone," Nick remarked.

"Won't be trappers, because there's no beaver," Travis said. "Might be an exploration party."

"Watch out, it could be Hudson's Bay agents," Martin ventured.

"That would be a problem, alright. Let's find out," Travis said as he reined the roan toward the smoke.

Drawing closer to the camp they could make out three men lounging in the shade beside the fire. They stopped short of the camp. "Hello the camp," Travis called out. "Can we come in?"

The three men stood up and looked toward them. "Come in," replied a voice strong in a French accent.

They dismounted, leading their horses up to the men. "We haven't seen anyone for days, and we were curious as to who you were," Travis said.

The three men studied Travis, Martin, and Nick. "Are you Hudson's Bay men?" asked the Frenchman.

"Should we be?" Travis asked.

"Hudson's Bay doesn't like anyone here who is not part of their company," the Frenchman replied.

"Are you part of their company?" Travis asked

The Frenchman snorted and laughed, but did not reply."

Nick and Martin exchanged glances, then Nick said to him, "We are not with Hudson's Bay, and we have no use for Hudson's Bay."

"You are not friends of Hudson's Bay, then," the Frenchman said.

"You can say that," Nick replied.

The Frenchman smiled, "I am Denis Fournier. What is your name?"

"Nick Dupre, originally from the Newcastle District of Rupert's Land." He gave a slight bow, "Coureur du Bois, at your service. No friend of Hudson's Bay. If you wish to arrest me, try your best."

Travis glanced at Martin, his eyes asking the question.

"Coureur du Bois, it means Runner of the Woods," Martin explained. "Hudson's Bay calls unlicensed trappers, *runners* because they run through the woods ahead of them."

The Frenchman chuckled, "I do not have that wish, runner of the woods."

The two men standing behind the Frenchman, one a few years older than the other, grew excited, and stepped up closer to Nick, to give him a better look. Then, they looked hard a Martin. The younger one, holding his eyes on Martin, asked, "Are you Monsieur Ouimette?"

Martin's eyes flared open in surprise, "Yes, I am Martin Ouimette. Do you know me?"

"We did not recognize you at first with the beard," the man said. "The last we saw, you had no beard, but my brother and I wondered." He turned to his brother, "I told you Monsieur Ouimette could not resist coming to the Rocky Mountains, he is a trapper, no?"

Martin looked closer at the two brothers, "Remi and Paul?"

Paul burst out laughing, "Yes! We are happy to see you!"

Nick's face held his surprise, "Remi and Paul Marier?" he asked.

Remi and Paul turned their attention, and smiles, to Nick. "Yes," Remi replied. "Do you remember us, Nick Dupre?"

Nick smiled, "Yes."

"We were friends together in the school," Remi exclaimed excitedly. "We got into trouble together from the school master, do you remember that?"

Nick laughed, "Which time?"

Remi laughed, "The best one! We let a skunk loose in the schoolroom so the master would close school, and we could go hunting."

Nick laughed, "He closed the school alright, but we didn't hunt that day. I can still feel the cane across my backside, and then my father added a few strokes, then he made me cut wood for a week."

Remi nodded, with a laugh. "I got the same punishment. Our fathers were friends, and I always believed they conspired on our punishment. We hunted together after that a lot. Then, your father and mother died," Remi quickly made the sign of the cross over his chest, "and you went away. We never saw you again."

"That is a long story, Remi," Nick replied, the smile fading away.

"You seem to be bound for somewhere now," Remi said. "Where?"

"Yes, we are," Nick replied. "We are bound for Fort Nex Perce."

"That is not a good place to go, if you are not with Hudson's Bay," Denis broke in.

"We have to go there," Martin said. "We are hunting a murderer, and he is ahead of us with four Hudson's Bay agents, and four horses of stolen pelts."

Remi gaped at Martin, "You were content to stay in St. Charles, I shudder to think of who he murdered that would make you leave your business, and come way out to this place."

"The man we hunt, is Duncan Black," Martin said. "He, along with a gang of cutthroats, broke into my house. They murdered my family. They thought they had killed me as well, but failed. We have been hunting them since St. Charles."

Remi and Paul stared at him in shock. "Mon Dieu!" Remi whispered. "That is horrible. I am so sorry, Monsieur Ouimette."

"Yes," Paul agreed. "I am sorry, as well."

"Where did the Hudson's Bay agents come from?" Denis asked.

"They were at the Pierre's Hole rendezvous," Martin answered. "They met with the murderers there, and left with them back this way. We were told they would go to Fort Nez Perce to sell the stolen pelts."

"Are you sure they have come this way?" Denis asked.

"We're on their trail, two of three days behind them," Travis said.

They all looked at Travis.

"This is our friend, Travis Walker," Martin said. "He has helped guide us to find the gang."

"Did the gang all flee to the Rocky Mountains?" Paul asked.

Martin nodded.

"Have you caught up to any of them, yet?" Denis asked.

"We have killed all but the one we follow," Nick replied. "He joined with the Hudson's Bay agents at Pierre's Hole. They protected him, and helped him escape us."

"How did you come to be with Mons . . .," Remi began to ask Nick.

Martin cut him off, "Please, it is easier to simply say, Martin."

Remi nodded, then asked Nick, "How did you come to be with Martin?"

"We are friends, and I came to help him hunt the men," Nick replied. "I had a good idea who they were."

Remi nodded, "There is a lot for us to catch up on, my old friend."

"Unfortunately, we don't have time to," Nick said. "We have to be after them."

"How much do you know about the country between here, and Fort Nez Perce?" Denis asked.

"Very little," Nick replied. "Except, where it is located, and that it's a Hudson's Bay fort."

"Then, you had better stay with us a while, and I will tell you about what you are headed into."

Nick looked at Martin, and Travis, "I think we should stay, and learn."

Martin nodded his agreement.

"That would be the smart thing to do," Travis replied. He looked at Denis, "Have you seen those five men, with five pack horses, four of them loaded with pelts? The man we hunt has a full red beard and long red hair."

"I have not," Denis replied. "I only joined with Remi and Paul yesterday. I was heading for the states to look for new trapping grounds.

"We saw them," Denis replied. "Two days ago, before Denis joined us. We were camped here, and they stopped. Four of the men said they were Hudson's Bay agents, and demanded to know what we were doing here. They asked for our licenses."

"Fortunately, Paul, and I, still have our licenses from the Newcastle District," Remi broke in. "They asked why we were out here, instead of there. I told him we had heard Hudson's Bay had good trapping here, so we came."

"Actually," Paul said with a grin, "we had no idea this was Hudson's Bay land until they said so. We just followed the Snake River looking for a place to trap."

"They left then," Remi said, "They were headed east along the river. There was a man with them, who said nothing, but looked evil as the devil himself. He had a red beard and long red hair."

"That's the man we hunt," Martin said. "Duncan Black."

"You have your work cut out for you, my friends," Denis said. "Taking him from the Hudson's Bay agents will not be easy. Especially, since you don't know the country."

"If he is a murderer, why is Duncan Black with the Hudson's Bay agents?" Paul asked.

"Because, he is a Hudson's Bay agent himself," Nick answered.

"He was a Hudson's Bay enforcer in the Red River Colony," Martin said. "He became a river pirate, killing and robbing. He, and his gang, fled out here after murdering my family. They employed an outlaw trapper to guide them. They killed trappers, and stole their pelts all the way here. He got in with the Bay agents, and he left with them, with the stolen pelts."

"So, they know he is a murderer, yes?" Denis asked.

"I told them," Travis answered. "I told the agents that, Black, and the outlaw trapper, were wanted for murders. They helped them escape anyway. Now, he's with them."

"So, that is why you are going to Fort Nez Perce, to catch him there," Denis said.

"Yes," Martin replied. "That is the one place we believe he will go. Have you been there?"

"I have trapped all this territory, and traded at Fort Nez Perce, and Fort Vancouver, for many years," Denis replied.

"Where is Fort Vancouver?" Travis asked Denis.

"Fort Vancouver is at the mouth of the Columbia River. It is the Hudson's Bay headquarters for the whole of the Columbia District. I have also been north into New Caledonia."

"You know this territory better than anyone else, then," Travis said.

"I know it very well," Denis replied. "It was good fur country, until the policy to kill all the beaver, and Hudson's Bay decided to pay even less for pelts than they did before. I was content to stay here until I was shorted on the sale of my pelts this spring. There is no reason for me to stay here, only to be cheated by Hudson's Bay. That's why I am headed for the rivers of the Rocky Mountains."

"We were following the river west, when Denis stopped at out camp yesterday," Remi said. "He told us to go back to the Rocky Mountains where the trapping was better. We were planning on going back tomorrow."

"The Rocky Mountain streams are being heavily trapped by the company trappers, and the beaver are thinning out," Travis said to them. "But, I know some places that are still good."

Paul looked at Remi and Denis, "Maybe we should join with them."

"We're not going back, yet," Travis said to him. "Once we finish what we came for, we will return. If you go on to the Rockies, maybe we will find you somewhere."

"I think we should help them," Paul said. "Find that man who did this horrible thing to Martin's family. We are only wandering anyway."

Remi looked at his brother for a moment, then nodded lightly, "Nick is our friend. Martin treated us fairly, and he is a good man. We should help them." Remi looked at Denis, "We can meet you somewhere later."

Denis held a displeased expression, then said, "I have been treated badly, and cheated, by Hudson's Bay. I would like very much to take some revenge on their agents, especially one who is a murderer, and protected by them."

"You're welcome in our party," Travis said. "It's always safer in numbers."

Denis looked at Travis, "I will guide you there."

"We could use a guide, if you want the job," Travis replied.

"Tend to your horses," Denis said. "Then, we will talk about it."

6

The six men sat together eating venison from a deer Paul had shot, drinking coffee, and exchanging stories about Hudson's Bay, and the encounters they had with them. Nick said no more about his past, than he had gone to live with his uncle after his parents died. Once grown he had gone back to the traplines as a coureur, learning to avoid the Hudson's Bay's agents.

Martin volunteered no details about the murders of his wife and children, and none dared ask. To pry into such a painful subject was beyond the right of any man, if Martin wanted to talk of it, they would listen. Remi did ask Martin, how he had come to know Duncan Black. He explained about the Red River Colony, the governor's decree against the Metis, and Black's role as an enforcer, and participant in the attack on the Metis at the battle of Seven Oaks.

Travis had been wondering at Remi's and Paul's last name. He finally asked, "Remi, Paul, are you related to Pierre Marier? He was in the Rocky Mountains trapping."

Remi nodded, "Yes, he is our uncle. We hoped to find him out here, we might find him yet."

Travis looked at Remi, deciding the best way to tell him the bad news. "Pierre was in the Rocky Mountains. He was well liked, all the trappers called him Frenchie Marier."

"You know him then!" Paul said excitedly. "Can you take us to him?"

Remi frowned, "You said, *was*."

Travis drew in a breath, and let it out, "Pierre is dead."

The faces on Remi and Paul sank in sorrow. "What happened to him?" Remi asked.

"He was murdered for his pelts by an outlaw trapper named Luther Monk."

Remi's face filled with scarlet rage, "I will find Luther Monk and kill him!"

Travis held up his hand, "Easy, Remi, let me finish. Monk was with another man, when they killed Frenchie. Four trappers, friends of mine, caught them in the act, and killed Monk's partner, but Monk escaped. He eventually came back to the mountains, guiding Duncan Black and his gang of cutthroats. He, along with Black, and the gang, murdered several of my friends and stole their pelts."

Remi, Paul, and Denis sat silent, listening to the account.

"Monk was with Black when the Hudson's Bay agents helped them escape us. We caught up to Monk on Henry's Fork, and we hanged him for his crimes. Black had a hand in killing my friends, just as he did Martin's family. Luther Monk is dead, but Duncan Black still has to pay for his crimes."

Remi's red face returned to its sun-browned color. He let out a breath, "At least he was punished for murdering our uncle."

"He was punished alright," Nick said. "He was terrified, and it was good that he knew such fear before he went to the devil."

"I can see why you pursue Duncan Black," Denis remarked. "He has to pay for his terrible crimes."

"No court under the rule of Hudson's Bay will punish him," Nick said with disgust. "They only punish men who trap without a license, or who they consider trespassers, but to a real criminal, they befriend him."

Denis angrily spit on the ground beside him in an act of contempt. "That is what I think of Hudson's Bay, they are all scoundrels."

"Denis," Travis began, "does the Snake go directly to the fort?"

"It does, but it wanders way to the north, then back down to where it empties into the Columbia. You do not want to go that route."

Travis furrowed his brow with concern, "Is there a different route?"

"There is, yes," Denis replied. He took a stick from the firewood pile. He drew a wavy line from east to west indicating the Snake River. He poked the stick into the line, "This is the great canyon, behind you," he dug the stick in deeper for the canyon."

"We came through it," Travis said.

"It is an ugly stretch, no?" Denis remarked.

"It wasn't the best country I've ever seen," Travis said.

Denis poked the stick in the line west of the canyon, "This is where we are now." He dragged the stick making the river longer, "We follow it so. Here it begins to curve to the north." He scratched a line, from the Snake to the west. "This is *Riviere Aux Malad*, it runs through a deep canyon."

"Not another canyon," Nick moaned.

"We do not go that far. It is how to mark the crossing."

"Good," Nick gave a sigh of relief.

"Why is it called the Sickly River?" Martin asked.

"Because, if you eat anything from it, or drink the water, you will become sick."

"Poison water?" Travis asked.

Denis shrugged, "Who knows, but I for one, am not interested in challenging the name to learn if it is so."

Travis nodded, "Go ahead, now which way?"

Denis poked the stick into the line, east of Sickly River, and dragged it across the river to the south side. "We cross the river here. It is the narrowest place on the river. It is too wide, and too deep, to swim horses across at any other place. If we do not cross here, we will be stuck on the north side, between the rivers Snake and Columbia. Both are too wide to swim horses, and the fort is on this side," he poked the stick on the south side of the Snake River. If you are on the north side of the Snake, you will not be able to get to the fort."

Travis looked up at Martin and Nick, "Guess, Tyler forgot about that, too. Good thing we met you, Denis. We would have stayed on this side of the river, and been stuck, and not able to reach the fort."

"The Snake gets wider as it gets closer to the Columbia, and the river Columbia is huge," Denis said. "You are on one side, or the other, if you have horses. If you have canoes like the Indians, then you can cross to and fro."

"Good to know," Travis remarked. "Okay, once we cross the river here, then, where do we go?"

Denis continued to scratch a line northward for the Snake. "We will cross four small rivers, easily waded, especially in summer." He scratched a line for each river, going north, "River Bruneau, river Great Rock, river Owyhee. After the river Owyhee, we begin to climb into the mountains. Then, we come to the fourth river, river Malheur."

"The river of misfortune," Nick said with a laugh. "I hope it's not an omen."

Travis looked at him.

"*Malheur* is French for misfortune," Nick explained.

"It is named so, because an explorer lost his cache there.

It is said the Indians stole it. So, he called it *Riviere Malheur,*" Denis remarked. He poked the stick into the Malheur River, and dragged a line northwest. "We go through the Blue Mountains here, then to the river Umatallow.

"It is flat, and some rolling hills." He drew a circle around the Umatallow River, taking in a wide area, "Anywhere in here, we could run into the Cayuse, and they can be unfriendly, but it is the best way to the fort."

He proceeded to draw in the Columbia running north and south, then westward. He drew a second line indicating the wide northern turn of the Snake, connecting it to the Columbia. He stabbed the stick in the spot previously marked, a short way down from the mouth of the Snake. "The fort is here."

"How is the trail over the Blue Mountains?" Travis asked.

"Good. The Nez Perce use it when going to the Columbia to trade."

"We were told to watch out for the Cayuse," Nick said. "How bad are they?"

"The Cayuse can be dangerous; they don't like the white trappers. Hudson's Bay men have angered them. We will have to be careful in their country. Beyond the Cayuse are the Wallawalla Indians." He made a large circle around the fort taking in the country east and south of it to the Columbia, "They are here, and they don't like white men much, either. They expect gifts from the white men to hunt and trap, even to fish. They know the Hudson's Bay men will trade with them, but expect much more than they get, and that makes them unhappy. Since we are not hunting or trapping, we should be okay with them. Like any Indian, be polite, but strong, and you will get by."

"Sounds like Hudson's Bay has made enemies," Travis remarked.

"Their methods create problems with the Indians, yes."

"They do the same in Rupert's Land," Martin said. "The only thing that saves Hudson's Bay there, is the Cree, Assiniboine, and Chippewa are not a hostile people. They expect the Indians to conform to their laws, most do not, but they do not fight either. The Cayuse and Wallawalla are not so peaceful to them."

Denis was looking at Martin as he spoke, then nodded lightly, "Tell them we are enemies of Hudson's Bay, and they might not attack."

"John Tyler was at the rendezvous with some other men," Travis said. "He told us the same thing about the Indians."

Denis smiled, "Yes, I know John. The last I saw him; he and his companions were going to the rendezvous with the Americans."

"He traded his pelts there, and said he was staying on the American side."

"Yes, that is what he said," Denis replied. "So, it is settled then. I can make my journey to the American streams later. Right now, I believe it is more important to put a stop to these criminals, and unless I guide you, your way will be lost, and they will escape."

"We appreciate that," Travis replied. "If you stay with us, I can set you up on a good trapping area."

Denis smiled, "That is a fair trade for our services."

THE FOLLOWING MORNING, they packed their horses, and left camp. Six riders, and three pack horses, could not be missed. They had only gone a few miles when a party of Shoshone rode toward them from the southwest. Travis and Denis were in the lead, they stopped to wait for the dozen Indians to come up.

Travis watched them, "That's Lean Otter," he said to the others. "He's a war chief, speaks English pretty good."

"Friend of yours?" Denis asked.

"Depends on the day," Travis replied.

The Shoshone stopped and looked over the horses and packs, Then, Lean Otter grinned at Travis, "Big Walker, you are far from your trapping grounds."

"We're not trappin'," Travis said. "We're huntin' down a man who killed friends of ours."

Lean Otter looked surprised, "You need six men, and three pack horses, to kill one man? Big Walker must be getting weak in his years. You killed many Cheyenne by yourself, and now you need all this help for one man?" He shook his head sadly, "The years have not been kind to you."

"Are the years kind to anyone?" Travis asked him.

Lean Otter shrugged, "To some, not to others. They are kind to me."

"We didn't start out like this," Travis said. He pointed at Martin and Nick, then himself, we started out after eleven men. We have killed ten, there is only one left, he is the one we hunt now." He pointed at Remi, Paul, and Denis, these are friends we met yesterday, and they wanted to come along."

Lean Otter stared at Travis. Travis could tell he was debating whether he was telling the truth about their killing ten men, or just saying that to make himself look bigger. Travis met his eyes, challenging him to say he was lying. If he did, they would fight. Lean Otter knew he could never beat the bear of a man.

"I take back what I said," Lean Otter remarked. "Big Walker has not become weak in his years."

Travis pointed at the three scalps hanging from Lean Otter's belt, "I see you haven't lost your strength, three Blackfoot scalps – good coups."

Lean Otter lifted his chin proudly, "I have many more on my lodgepole." He gave Travis the same challenging look, daring him to call him a liar."

"I believe you," Travis said. "You have always been a warrior."

"You had better go now, or you will never catch your last man," Lean Otter said.

Travis waved at him, as he heeled his horse forward. The others followed. The Shoshone watched them for several minutes, then went on their way.

"It looked like you two were having a duel," Nick remarked to Travis.

"We were. He was making fun of me for having this many men to hunt down one man. He was thinking about calling me a liar when I said we had already killed ten men. He knew better. He knew I'd snap his neck like a dry twig, but he had to save his pride with the party, so he accepted my story, and complimented me. It was now my turn to compliment him for his compliment, or he would have been insulted, giving him the right to kill me. I blew out his fuse by pointing out the scalps, and complimenting him. He saw an opportunity to turn the table, and put me on the spot, by saying he had many more scalps. If I said, or did, anything indicating I didn't believe him, they would have killed us all. I said, I believed him, and that resolved the standoff."

"I thought we had good relations with the Shoshone," Martin said.

"As well as you can with any Indian," Travis replied. "They like to fight. Today he was feelin' a little quarrelsome, tomorrow he'd be my best friend, the next day he's in a sour mood, and everyone is his enemy – including me."

"The customs are complex, you just have to know what to say," Martin surmised.

"That's exactly it," Travis replied. "What to say, and *how* to say it, will keep your scalp attached to your skull."

"How far to the Malheur River?" Nick asked Denis.

"Two days, unless Travis gets into more compliment contests with his Indian friends," Denis replied with a grin.

Travis grinned back, "Well, if we do, I'll try and keep it short."

"Not too short," Martin said. "I would like to keep my scalp attached to my skull."

7

The Malheur River proved to be a narrow, slow-moving stream, brown in color, the slower stretches green with water algae from the summer heat. The banks, down to the water line, were covered in thick green grass and plant growth. Willow was prominent along the banks, overshadowed by cotton-woods, and a variety of green-leaf trees.

They stopped at the bank and looked the stream up and down. The willows showed heavy beaver cutting, but it was all old. Nowhere were the pointed stubs of trunks, cut by beaver teeth, showing fresh and white. The banks were littered with sticks stripped clean of bark that had once fed beaver, but the waterway was void of any fresh cuttings. In the distance, a beaver dam had collapsed from lack of reconstruction.

"That fur desert policy of the Bay has sure done the job," Travis remarked with a bitter tone. "This stream should be loaded with beaver, but nothing. The grass banks are perfect for muskrats, but I don't see any work from them either."

Denis nodded, "They have wiped out the streams flowing into the river Snake. Then, they think we should stay and trap for them, and come to the fort with two beaver plews, and a muskrat for a winter's work."

"They can't be taking in much fur then," Nick remarked. "How can they afford to keep Nez Perce open?"

"To the northwest, southwest, and west, they have not wiped out the fur. To the northwest, the lands of the Cowlitz, Nisqually, and Clickitat Indians, and to the west and southwest of here, in the valleys of the Callapooya, Moollalla, and Umpqua Indians, the streams are still loaded with beaver. They just want to create a stretch of land where no fur animal exists, but this is the area they want us to keep trapping, and it is no good for us."

Crossing the Malheur they turned to the northwest, riding through hilly country, barren of trees. Grass, brown from the heat, waved in the breeze, sagebrush ranging from basket to tree size, dotted the hillsides. The further north they rode, the steeper the climbing became, yet, unlike the tree covered passes of the Rocky Mountains, with creeks and streams in abundance, this country was arid, and water did not exist.

The gait of the horses was slowing by the hour as they

grew weary and thirsty. The men followed the lowest draws to save the horses, however, the steepness of ascending and descending the hills, was taking its toll on them.

"Rest the horses," Denis called out. We have another big hill to climb."

They stopped, and dismounted. Resetting the saddles, and packs, that shifted during the climbing, the men then sat on the ground holding the reins and lead ropes, allowing the horses to graze on the brown grass.

"How long does this climbin' go on?" Travis asked Denis. "The horses are wearin' down."

Denis pointed to a bare ridgeline ahead of them, "See that ridge?"

Travis squinted his eyes at it, "Yeah, looks like about two hours away."

"About that, yes. Once we top that, we go downhill. The river Snake comes back to the trail at the bottom. We can camp there, rest the horses, and give them water."

Travis looked up at the sun, "Be about sunset when we get to the river. Would those Bay agents have come this way?"

"They have to, it is the only way to reach the fort from this side," Denis replied.

"Could they leave their horses on the north side of the river, and take boats across to the fort?" Nick asked.

Denis shook his head, "The fort is six miles from the Snake, they would need them, to pack the pelts, or they would have to walk and carry them. Besides, there is no place to leave the horses there. They have to come this way."

"If it is impossible to get across the river to Fort Nez Perce, where do the trappers on the other side trade their pelts?" Martin asked.

"They go to Fort Vancouver, or take canoes across the Columbia to Fort Nez Perce to trade, then go back."

"You are right, they have no choice but to go this way, and they have to go as slowly as we do," Martin said. "That keeps them from gaining extra days on us."

Denis looked at him, "You can only go so fast on this pass, or the horses will die under you. It is a long way to walk, carrying their food, and pelts."

Martin nodded, "They would never abandon four horse loads of pelts."

"We are behind them, true," Denis said, "however, we know where that are going."

"I wonder if they've figured out we're following them?" Nick asked.

"Hard to say," Travis replied. "If they have, they figure they can sell the pelts, and be gone before we get there."

"The Bay agents are arrogant," Denis remarked. "Even if they did know we follow, they would believe they are superior to us, and we are not a threat. They always think they are wiser and better than everyone else."

They fell to silence, resting as best they could on the shadeless ground. When they saw the horses had stopped

eating, and relaxing into sleep, they mounted and
rode on.

Reaching the crest of the grade, the Snake River lay
before them, as did miles of flat land between the brown
hills. Nick took out the spyglass, and studied the miles of
open country ahead of them while they rested the horses
from the climb. The rest of them checked the saddles and
packs.

Travis walked up beside Nick, "See anything?"

"There is a camp by the river, looks like three men,"
Nick replied.

"Any of them have red hair?" Travis asked.

"Can't tell from here, but I only see three men, not five,
but the other two could be behind the trees."

Denis walked up to them, "What do you see?"

"A camp with three men, by the river," Nick answered.

"Could be Hudson's Bay trappers," Denis said. "We will
see when we go down there."

Mounting the horses, they began the descent to the
river.

"We will have some miles of flat land before we start
climbing again," Denis called out to the group.

A half hour later they reached the river, the banks
covered in willow, and long grass. Riding through the sage
and juniper they took the anxious horses directly to the
water, they dismounted to let the animals drink. A short
way downstream, the smoke from the campfire Nick had

spotted from the ridgetop, rose into the air from a clearing among the juniper trees.

They were all looking at the smoke when, Remi said to Travis, "Paul and I will go talk to them, see who they are. If they are the agents, we have our licenses, and if it is Duncan Black, he won't know us."

"Go ahead," Travis replied.

Remi and Paul left their horses with the others, and walked along the bank to the camp. Remi called to the camp as he neared, "Hello, can we come in to talk to you?"

A voice called back, "Come in."

Remi, whispered to his brother, "While I talk, you be looking around to see if there are other men. It looks like they have been here a long time, though."

Paul nodded, "I see only three men, but five horses. There would have to be pack horses, so three men should be right. There is meat hanging from the trees. They did not just get here."

"Good day," Remi called out to the men as they entered the camp.

"Good day, the men all returned. "Can we help you?" one asked.

"My name is Remi, and this is my brother Paul. We, and some friends, just came from up river."

"I'm Baptiste," he pointed to the others, Henry, and Louis."

"We are looking to catch up with some Hudson's Bay

agents, have you seen them?" Remi asked. "There are five men, and five pack horses."

"Yes, they passed this way two days ago," Baptiste replied. "Five men, who said they were Hudson's Bay agents, and asked for our licenses. We showed them, and they were satisfied. We are trappers for Hudson's Bay, so we had no problems."

"We are as well," Remi said. "Did one of the agents have a big red beard, and long red hair?"

"Yes, one was. We thought it strange, because he did not look at all like the other four, who were agents. We have seen enough Hudson's Bay officials to recognize them. That one, we were not so sure about."

"They had five pack horses, four were loaded with pelts," Henry said. "They said they bought them at the American rendezvous on the Teton River."

"Yes, there was a rendezvous up there. Have you been camping here long?" Remi asked.

"We were assigned to trap the Snake River this past winter, and this spring, but there are very few beaver left on it, or any fur, for that matter," Baptiste replied with a hint of bitterness. "We traded the few pelts we had at Fort Nez Perce, and were told to come back here to trap. We are not happy about this, because there is nothing here to trap. We will make nothing."

"Do you know why they are making you trap here?" Remi said.

The three men looked at him with interest. "Why?" Louis asked.

"The Bay is trying to kill every fur animal in this area to keep the Americans from coming over here to trap. If there is no fur, they will not come."

"Is that why they are forcing us to stay here?" Baptiste snapped.

"Yes. They are afraid the Americans will come, and trap the northern areas, and New Caledonia, so they are creating a fur desert here. It is by the order of Governor Simpson, we are told."

The three men exchanged angry looks. "We are being used for their politics," Baptiste snarled. Henry and Louis nodded in agreement.

"You should go to the American side and trap," Remi said.

"We have been discussing that," Baptiste replied. "Now, what you have told us, has convinced us to go. We will leave tomorrow."

"Are you going all the way to Fort Nez Perce?" Henry asked.

"If we have to," Remi replied.

"Why, if you have no pelts to trade?" Louis asked.

"That man with the red beard led a gang that murdered a woman, and two children, in St. Charles. They also killed trappers, and stole their pelts. They did not trade for those pelts at the rendezvous, they lied. Those pelts were stolen from trappers they murdered. The red beard is a Hudson's Bay enforcer from the Red River Colony, and the agents are protecting him from the men who hunt him. They will go to the fort to sell the pelts. We hope to catch them there."

The three men looked at each other, "We knew he was a reprobate when we saw him," Baptiste remarked. "I hope you find them."

"We will," Remi replied. "Maybe we will see you at the next rendezvous."

"I'm sure you will. We have had enough of this bad business!" Baptiste said with conviction. "Before you leave, I will give you a warning. The Cayuse up on riviere Umatallow, are angry with Hudson's Bay, and have killed two trappers, maybe more. Be careful of them."

"Thank you for the warning," Remi said. "We will be careful. We will let you get back to your plans to leave. We just wanted to ask if you saw the agents." They turned back toward where the others waited.

The men were staking the watered horses in patches of grass, when Remi and Paul returned. They all came back around the brothers. "What did you learn?" Nick asked them.

"They are Hudson's Bay trappers," Remi answered, "or, were. They have been ordered to trap the Snake until all the beaver are gone, they are catching nothing of course. They are quitting, and heading for the American side."

"Did they see the agents?" Travis asked.

Remi nodded, "They stopped by their camp two days

ago. They described Duncan Black accurately, and there were five of them, and four pack horses carrying pelts. The agents demanded to see their licenses."

"They thought Black looked like a reprobate, and not an agent," Paul added.

"They weren't wrong there," Nick remarked.

Martin snorted with disdain, "How moral, and ethical, of them. They protect a child murderer, and carry stolen pelts that men were murdered for, but they check to make sure honest trappers have their proper pieces of paper. The utter hypocrisy of these men knows no bounds."

"Corrupt men have no bounds," Travis said. "You will find them everywhere, and the more unchecked power they are given, the more corrupt they become. We will find a way to take Black from their protection."

"We were given a warning," Paul broke in. "He said, the Cayuse are angry with Hudson's Bay, and killed two trappers, perhaps more."

Denis snorted, "Such a surprise, that the Bay is making enemies among the Indians."

"Killing all the fur the Indians need for trade might have something to do with that," Nick remarked.

"Did they say where the Cayuse were attacking?" Denis asked.

"Along the Umatallow River," Paul answered.

Denis nodded, "That is what I said before. The river Umatallow is where we might meet them, and now they are unhappy. We will have to be cautious."

"We survived attacks from the Cheyenne, and Blackfeet, we can the Cayuse, too, Nick remarked.

"I'd rather just avoid 'em, if we can," Travis said. "We need to stay close to Black."

"We will not know until we get there,' Martin said. "We will deal with what comes."

Travis looked at Martin, "You're learnin' how this country runs. We plan, but are not locked into the plan. When things change, we have to change with them. That's how it is with everything out here. Don't borrow worries, just deal with the moment when it comes."

"Sound advice," Denis remarked.

"Now, let's get a fire goin'," Travis said. "I could use some coffee, and food."

"Paul and I will go hunt some meat," Remi said. "They picked up their rifles and headed downriver.

THE NEXT DAY they started out with easy travel over miles of flat land. By noon the grade began to steepen, and stayed that way until they made camp in an open area of grass. A small creek provided water, and grass along its banks for the exhausted horses.

In the morning, with the horses rested, watered and fed, they continued to climb. They came on several stretches of flat land where the horses could ease their strained breathing, and tired muscles. As they approached each new climb, they stopped and rested the horses, before proceeding. The strain of miles of climbing was showing on the animals in their slowed pace, sweat drenched bodies, and lowering heads and ears.

Around them rose the peaks of the Blue Mountains. Denis said they earned their name from their blue appearance cast by the dense growth of evergreen trees on the slopes. By the end of the day, the barren, brown hills had evolved into pine, fir, and aspen covered mountains. On a crystal-clear stream, with a wide expanse of green grass, shaded with aspen and fir, they made camp. Here they stayed for an extra day to rest the horses.

After two days, with the horses rested, and well fed, they continued the climb through the timbered mountains. Here the air was cooler than the arid country behind them. Water was not scarce, and grass was plentiful. As the day wore on, the pass grew steeper requiring more rest stops for the horses. Suddenly, they topped out on the pass, before them lay level ground covered in fir and pine. They stopped, dismounted, and let the horses rest.

"Are we through the worst of it?" Travis asked Denis.

"This is the top of the pass," Denis said. "We will be going downhill for a long way now. The climbing from here on will be little hills, not hard on the horses."

After a rest, they rode across the level stretch, then began to descend on a gentle grade. They came to a clearing that overlooked a vast area below them. Here, Nick used his spyglass to make a thorough study of the area. The others waited patiently as his spent several minutes looking. He eventually lowered the glass. "I see deer and elk, but no men."

"They are several days ahead of us, they would be past that country by now," Denis said.

Nick put the glass away, "You never know what you'll see until you look. They probably took resting days like we did."

Denis nodded, "You are right. They could have stopped, and we would be close behind, and you would see them."

They continued down the grade. Nick stopped on occasion to glass the country. On one stop, he said, "I can see the treeline of a creek, and beyond it, the treeline of a river. What river is that?"

Denis rode up beside Nick, "That would be the river Umatallow." He held out his hand, Nick gave him the glass. Denis studied the country. "That is the river, and all looks as usual." He lowered the glass and gave it back to Nick. He looked at the others as they waited, "We should camp by that creek tonight. Rest the horses. Tomorrow we will cross the river Umatallow, and there we will run the risk of the Cayuse."

8

In the morning they set off following the creek toward the Umatallow River. Travis's eyes were ever roving, searching intently over the country for Indians. He figured there was no difference between these Cayuse, attacking on open ground, and the Cheyenne doing the same. He pulled one rifle and laid it across the saddle in front of him, as he stretched his senses into the wind.

Martin and Nick, having experienced Indian attacks, and now knowing what to watch for, copied Travis. Remi and Paul looked at them with curiosity.

Nick saw them looking. "We learned in the Rocky Mountains to be on guard for Indian attacks. If the Cayuse are looking for a fight, we have to be able to respond quickly, so the rifles are kept at the ready."

Paul looked at his brother, "We have much to learn, yet." He pulled his Hawken, and laid it across the saddle. Remi did as well."

"I will keep my rifle cased," Denis said. "I will talk to them if we have an encounter. Me, not having a gun out, will show them we will talk, but you having your guns ready, shows them, we will fight."

With the river's treeline in sight, they stopped and studied the open country around them. Nick studied the trees through the glass, then took it down. "I can't see the other side of the river for the trees."

Moving on, they reached the edge of the river, and stopped. "Water the horses," Denis said. "It is four or five hours to the next water."

"Fill your bellies and canteens," Travis said to the group. "If we get pinned down for a fight, you will need that water."

The men dismounted, the river was summer-shallow with numerous sand and rock bars exposed between the channels of water. They let the horses drink, filled their canteens, and drank for themselves. Once the horses were satisfied, they crossed the river at a bend that swung deeply toward them, and into the covering trees on the north side.

They moved through the trees, then stopped at their edge before riding out onto the open, treeless landscape. Nick took out his spyglass and scoured the country from left to right, in a slow half-circle search for Indians. With the naked eye, the men could see, to their north, northeast, and northwest. The land ran in flat, grass covered prairie with swells rolling like a dry sea. To their east was a rugged range of foothills, studded with firs and leaf trees. Between them and the range, the land held a series of hills with deep draws choked with trees and brush.

"What do you see?" Travis asked Nick.

"A lot of very empty land," Nick replied without taking the glass from his eye. He moved his horse out from the trees a few yards to get a better look to his right. "There's rough hills this way, draws filled with trees," he called back.

"Could you hide a war party in there?" Travis asked.

"You could hide a couple dozen in there," Nick replied.

Travis moved his horse out beside Nick. "Let me have a look."

Nick handed him the glass. Travis took it and studied the hills along the river. He then lowered the glass and stared out to the north. "That's a lot of open country to be caught in. No cover for a fight."

"They probably know that, and wait like a fox over a mousehole, for someone to ride out there," Nick remarked.

Travis frowned as he studied the terrain, "That's what I'm worried about." He turned around, "Denis, come out here."

Denis heeled his horse to move up beside Travis.

"Point out the trail to the fort," Travis said to him.

Denis pointed to the north, and ran his finger to the northeast, "There is no actual trail, but that is the direction."

"Is it all open like this?"

"Yes, but it's easy travel, and we could make the fort in a day."

Travis nodded his acknowledgement, then added, "Providing the Cayuse don't kill us first."

"That is a concern," Denis agreed. "There is no cover. If we get caught out there, we have no defense, and we can't outrun their horses with pack horses."

"That line of hills to the right, if we follow along it, keeping close to cover, how far off track will that put us, if we stick to that route?"

"We can follow the river for a short way, but then it will curve back into the mountains, and away from the fort. If we follow the edge of the hills, we will come out where the next water is, but it will add a day to our travel, without water."

Travis furrowed his brow, "Go without water for two days, or risk the Cayuse."

"The Cayuse can still attack by the hills."

"Yeah, but at least we'll have cover," Travis replied. "How far is it from that water to the fort?"

"It is a straight shot north, about five hours."

"How long will we be by this river before we divert off from it?" Travis asked.

"An hour before it curves away."

"Nick," Travis said, "How does that hill line look for travel and cover?"

Nick turned the glass to his right. "Hilly, but not bad.

Plenty of cover for defense."

"Then, we're going to follow the hills to the water, then go north from there," Travis said.

Denis nodded, "It will work out. A little more time, but it is the safer way to go."

They turned back to the other three waiting in the trees. Travis explained what they were going to do, and why. All were in agreement it was the wisest plan. They moved the horses out of the trees and followed the river east.

Riding with all the men alert, an hour passed before the river curved to the south, leaving them riding along the base of the hills away from the river. Travis and Denis were in the lead, when Travis suddenly pulled up his horse. A line of Indians was riding down from a fir covered hillside, their path would bring them onto the flats a stone's throw to their front. The group stopped, watching to see where the Indians were going.

The line of Indians kept coming out of the trees, Travis counted twenty-three mounted, and armed Indians. "Are those Cayuse?" he asked Denis.

"Yes."

The lead riders turned their heads to look right and left, and saw Travis' party. They began to point and talk, bringing the attention of all the Indians to them. They changed direction, and began riding toward them. Another ten Indians, that had been hidden from view, followed them."

"That puts it six-to-one," Travis said to Denis. "Let's see how good you can parley."

They held their places, but Travis was looking for the best escape route to cover if it came down to a fight. The river was not that far behind them, they could make the cover of the trees if they pushed the horses.

The Cayuse rode directly up to them, then stopped, forming a half circle around the group. They didn't say anything, but their combined interest was on the pack horses. They saw the rifles at the ready, and eyed them as well.

Travis studied them. Ten, including the leader, had British style rifles. Long barreled, and awkward, poor in a fight. The others carried bows, with quivers of arrows at their sides. They looked similar to the Nez Perce, but had fuller faces. All had their hair in long braids, with beaded tokens holding them. A few wore cloth shirts that had to come from white traders, others wore no shirts, or vests of tanned hide. They were mounted on horses smaller than the ones they rode, a mix of colors, bay, sorrel, pinto, and brown. The men weren't painted for war, so it wasn't a war party, but they weren't hunting either. A patrol looking for trespassers, and they had found some.

Denis began the communication with some basic signs of greeting to the patrol chief.

The chief, using signs, and a few words, replied, "What are you doing here?"

Denis replied, in a similar use of Cayuse words and

signs, "We are only passing through. We are not hunting or trapping."

The chief gave him a skeptical look, "Why do you have so many men, and pack horses, if you are only passing through?"

Denis pointed at Martin, "We are trailing the man who killed his wife and children."

The Cayuse all looked at Martin.

The chief huffed a cynical laugh, "All of you are hunting one man?" Several of the Indians laughed.

Denis pointed at Martin, Nick, and Travis, "It was only those at first. They hunted eleven men. They have killed all but the one we still hunt. They are warriors. They have given us the honor to ride with them to watch them kill the last man."

The Indians looked at the three men indicated; their laughter stopped at the hard-eyed, stern faces, Travis, Martin, and Nick gave them.

The Indians studied the six men, their eyes clearly coveting the rifles, and pack horses.

Denis continued, "The man we hunt is with four Hudson's Bay men."

"Hudson Bay!" the chief spit on the ground. He shook his head, with a scowl.

"You do not like Hudson Bay?" Denis asked.

The chief angrily spun his hand signs, and adding Cayuse words, replied, "We do not trust them. They are trespassers, and thieves. They steal the fur."

"We do not trust them either. The man, who is with them, that we want, has a red beard, the color of a robin's breast? Have you seen the man with the red beard?"

"No."

"We would like to go on to find him. We will leave your land when we have caught this killer."

The chief waved them on. "Go. Kill the Hudson Bay men."

Denis thanked him, and moved his horse forward. The others followed him without a word, as the Cayuse watched them ride on.

"Don't anyone look back at them." Travis said. "Keep your eyes forward."

"Why?" Paul asked.

"If we look back, they'll think we're scared of 'em," Travis answered.

They rode in silence, then Travis asked Denis, "I could pick up on some of that, but not all."

"He hates Hudson's Bay," Denis said. "I told him we were hunting the red beard man, and would leave when we killed him. They agreed to let us go."

"Why were they laughing," Martin asked.

"Because we are so many men, and pack horses, to hunt down one man."

"Just like the Shoshone did," Martin remarked.

"They think we are weak because we fear one man so much it takes all of us to get him," Travis explained. "That's how Indians think."

"I told them, the three of you were warriors, and had already killed ten of the men. You were giving us the honor or riding with you to watch you kill the last man," Denis said.

"That's when they stopped laughin'," Travis remarked.

"Yes, they weren't sure if it was worth attacking six men, three who were warriors," Denis added.

"They were showing a lot of interest in the pack horses," Nick said.

"Yeah, and the rifles," Travis agreed, "too much interest. We have a lot of good truck, and guns, for the taking."

"With the fur being wiped out, the Indians have nothing for trade at the fort for things they want," Denis said. "Trappers have all of that, which explains why they are killing trappers."

"Think they will come back for us?" Martin asked.

"Yes," Travis replied. "We have too much for them to pass up." He glanced over his shoulder to see if the Indians were still watching them. He saw the last of the Cayuse ride back into the hills they had just come down. "Okay, they all just rode back into the hills."

"They just came out of the hills, why would they go back?" Paul asked.

"To get ahead, and take us in an ambush," Nick answered.

Travis studied the hills, "But, where?"

They rode on, everyone searching the terrain for any sign of attack. A quarter hour passed before Travis stopped his horse, and studied a wide, tree filled draw ahead of them. His roan, accustomed to the smell of Indian horses as herd mates, snapped his head up. Ears pinned forward, nostrils flared open, the roan let out a whinny. A horse called back.

Travis abruptly jerked the roan to the right, and kicked him into a run for the trees. The others followed without question. The first war cries sounded as they reached the trees. The Indians had set an ambush in the draw, but the horses had prematurely tripped the trigger.

They hit the trees at a dead run, the packs bouncing wildly on the pack horses. Martin and Nick, now consummate Indian fighters, knew what to do. Jumping from the horses, they held the reins, as they each fired their first shot at the wall of Indians coming at them. Two Indians pitched from their horses, hitting the dry ground in a puff of dust. Travis dropped a third.

The Indians broke off the attack. "Tie the horses to trees!" Travis shouted out.

Martin and Nick had their horses tied, and their second rifles out. They stood watching as they reloaded the first ones.

Remi and Paul tied their horses, then stood, showing their confusion at the sudden attack. They had their guns out, but had not fired at the attackers. Nick looked at them, they were clearly at a loss for what to do. He shouted at them, to get their attention, "Remi! Paul! Wake up! That was just the first attack, they'll be back. When they come again, shoot them! Just holding your guns isn't helping."

Travis looked at the two, "How did you get this far without an Indian fight?" he asked them.

"We never had any trouble," Remi said.

"Well, you got trouble now," Travis said. You're goin' to cut your Indian fightin' teeth today. Nick, help 'em."

"I got them," Nick replied.

"They could come from any direction," Nick told Remi and Paul. "Listen with your ears. Look with your eyes. If you see an Indian, aim, and shoot him dead."

"Why are they attacking us?" Paul asked him. "They said we could go."

"They want what's in our packs, and our guns. Guns are hard to come by for Indians," Nick replied. "They know now, it's not going to be easy to get them. The ambush failed. A direct charge got three of them killed. They have to try something different. It might be another charge from all directions, or they might try sneaking up on us. If you fire your rifle, and they're close on you, drop it, and pull your knife, and don't be afraid to use it. Now, pay attention."

Travis looked at them, "Listen to Nick, he's a good Indian fighter."

Nick grinned at Travis, "I learned from the best."

Travis snorted, "Let's hope the *best* rides away from this one."

The second rush of Indians came without a sound.

Suddenly there was a swarm of them in the trees. All six men fired at the one closet to him. Four fell and didn't move, two others fell, but got back up, they retreated holding their wounds. The attack broke off.

"They are not like the Blackfeet, who just keep coming," Martin said.

"I guess the Cayuse like to hit and run," Travis said.

"Except, there are fewer running away each time," Denis remarked.

"That's the idea," Travis came back.

They all fell to silence, listening and watching. Fifteen minutes passed slowly, then thirty, and forty. The day grew hotter, but the shade of the trees made it tolerable. The breeze rustled the leaves, the gathering flies created a buzz as they swarmed over the blood of the dead men. The river was a hundred yards behind them, trees and brush filled the space between the water and them.

A strong breeze blew through, rattling the leaves in the trees, and picking up the dead, dry leaves, and skittering them across the ground. The wind whipped around in a circle, catching the smell of the water, and passing it through the trees. It also brought the smell of the Indians. Travis' acute sense of smell picked up the scent, as did the roan, whose attention turned toward the river.

Travis peered through the trees, then without a word, shouldered the Hawken, and fired. The shot snapped the attention of the others to him. Realizing Travis was facing the river, they looked to their rear. Martin and Nick, brought their rifles up and fired. Denis looked to his right, and fired.

Remi looked to his left, raised the rifle and fired.

A sudden flash of movement burst from the trees and careened into Paul. His rifle falling to the ground as he somersaulted from the blow. He looked up to see an Indian making to leap on him with a knife in his hand. Instinctively, Paul kicked the Indian's feet out from under him, causing him to take a hard face-plant in the leaves and dirt. Paul scrambled to his feet, yanking out his knife, he landed his knees on the Indian's back, and sunk the knife to the hilt between his shoulder blades. The Indian shuddered, then went limp. Paul jumped to his feet, and grabbed up his rifle, quickly looking around.

Remi hurried to his brother, "Are you hurt?"

Paul shook his head, slightly trembling.

"Take your knife from his back, you might need it again," Remi said.

Paul pulled the knife from the Indian's back. He stared at the bleeding hole for a second, then wiped the knife in the leaves, and sheathed it.

Travis walked up to Paul, and slapped him on the back, "Now, you're an Indian fighter. We're not done, yet, so pay attention."

Paul nodded. Checking his gun, he found the cap had been knocked off the nipple in the crash of bodies. He quickly put another one in place, and stood ready, scanning the trees.

Travis walked past Nick, "He'll do."

The morning turned to noon, and an hour past it. No more attacks came, yet they remained in the cover, their attention on every movement and sound.

Travis walked up beside Denis, "What do you think? I'm used to Blackfeet and Cheyenne, and how they fight. These, Cayuse, if they get shot-up enough, do they quit?"

"I don't know," Denis replied. "I've had fights with other Indians, but this is the first time I've had a fight with Cayuse."

"They've probably never run into a group of experienced Indian fighters before," Travis said. "Killin' a couple of trappers by surprise ain't the same thing."

"I think we scared them," Denis said. "They thought we were weak, and they wanted our property. They didn't expect to get half their party killed trying for it. They have to go back to the village, and explain their actions to the chiefs, and tell the widows why their husbands got killed trying to steal some coffee and blankets."

"Pretty expensive coffee," Travis remarked. "Do you know the way in the dark?"

Denis nodded, "We should have a good moon, the sky is clear, it's open country. If we go a little west of north from here, we will come to the next water, then on to the Columbia."

"Okay. Let's water the horses, and as soon as its dark, we'll get out of here, and ride all night."

9

Night fell as they continued their watch for another Indian attack, but it never came. "Water the horses, and let's make our move," Travis said.

They led the horse to the river, let them drink, filled their canteens, and rode out of the trees. Through the night, Denis led them in a northwest direction up and down the rolling hills. The moon and stars reflected off the light color of the sand and grass, while giving them direction. The night was cool, making travel easier on horses and men.

Travis could read his direction by the stars, but without Denis guiding them, he would have been lost. The country looked all the same, whether in moonlight, or sunlight. There was nothing distinguishing to use as landmarks, as everywhere he looked the land was the same. If he was to close his eyes, turn in circles, then open his eyes, he would have no idea where he was, or what direction to go in. This was not country to his liking, and he was anxious to be out of it, and back to the Rocky Mountains.

Every few hours they stopped to rest the horses. There were no streams, or even a pothole of water to be found, however, the cool night kept the horses from becoming exhausted due to thirst. Travis considered how terrible it would have been if they had stayed to the north side of the Snake. They would have gone through all this miserable country, only to find themselves trapped on the north side of the Snake, unable to reach the fort, or Duncan Black.

THE SUN WAS RISING as they topped another hill. The blue and pink of the sunrise spread over the low hills behind them. To the west, they could see a long line of trees projecting above the flat landscape. "There is the water," Denis said, pointing to the trees.

They rode on to the treeline. A trickle of water, two inches deep, flowed at the bottom of the creek bed. The eroded banks, and debris caught two-feet up in the trees, indicated how high the creek got during the spring thaw, or flash floods from a heavy rain. Now, in the heat of summer, it was a trickle, but a trickle it was. Water for horses and men.

Dismounting, they led the horses into the near-dry creek bed, and let them drink. They were all exhausted from the long ride, lack of sleep, and energy sapped from them by the fight with the Cayuse.

"How much further?" Martin asked.

"Half a day," Denis replied.

"We can all use a little sleep, and the horses need a longer rest," Travis said. "We'll stay here for a few hours before moving on."

All were in agreement. Once the horses had drank, they staked them on the grass to graze. They removed the packs from the horses, but left all the saddles on. Four would sleep for an hour, while two guarded, then rotate them into sleep.

Just before the sun was at its full, noon height, they mounted, and rode on. The hours passed as the glare of the afternoon sun filled the cloudless blue sky, and turned the flat land into an oven. Although it was an intense heat, it was a dry heat that brought little sweat out of the men or horses.

It was late afternoon when Denis pointed to the west, "That is the last ridge, from the top you can see the river Columbia."

An hour later, they topped the ridge. Stopping, they looked to the open space before them, the scene was dominated by the wide Columbia River below. Beyond it was more of the same terrain as they were in. The bottom of the hill ran out over a flat stretch of

protruding rock, short brown grass, with sagebrush to
the river's edge.

Riding down the hill, they came to the flat ground.
Moving toward the water, they found the bank rocky, and
dropping off abruptly into the deep river. They had to fight
the horses to keep them from running for the water, and
plunging off into the river. They had to ride another mile
before coming to a place the horses could stand spraddle-
legged, and reach their muzzles down into the water. The
men drank, and filled their canteens. Standing on the bank
they could see Indians in canoes on the river.

Travis looked upriver to where rugged bluffs came
down to the water. There was no passage between them
and the river. "Looks like we have to go up and around
those."

"We will," Denis replied. "It's the last hills we have to
climb, though. That stretch of bluffs will run for a mile or
so, but then we can drop back down to the river."

They rode to the top of the bluff, a vantage point giving
them a magnificent view in all directions. The wind blew
strongly across the bluff, bending the grass to the ground,
and forcing them to squint their eyes against it. Denis
pointed to the north, "See where the river grows wide, and
bends inland? That is called the, Great Bend, the fort is on
that bend."

Nick had his spyglass out studying the land ahead. "I see
the fort. There's a river before it, and there is a bridge
over it."

"That is the river Walula," Denis answered. "There is no good graze for the fort's horses near the fort. They are taken to the river for grazing. A small bridge was built over the river to take the horses to grass. We are almost there." He moved his horse on, the others following.

The high bluffs ended, and below them the land expanded out to flat ground. Tall grass bent in the wind, and trees dotted the landscape. Dropping down into a draw, they followed it out onto the flat land that ran to the shore of the Columbia.

Crossing the bridge over the Walula River, they saw the fort's horses grazing. "How come the Indians haven't stolen those horses?" Travis asked Denis.

"The Wallawalla Indians are a river tribe, they use few horses," Denis answered. "Their travel is mostly by canoe, and they eat what the river, and area around it, provides. Salmon is a main food for them. They don't need horses enough to steal them."

The closer they drew to the fort, the more the flat land expanded. The eastern hills appeared to be no more than rolling mounds in the distance. Due to the open land, the wind swept over them like a gale, picking up the fine sand and blasting them with it. They had to peer through half-closed eyes to prevent being blinded by the fine sand. Ahead of them, the structure of the fort took shape.

The fort showed new construction on the palisade walls, a bastion was positioned on the northeast and southwest corners. Gates were on the east and west walls. What was inside could not be seen.

"As of last year, Simon McGillivray, is the Post Master," Denis said. "He has done considerable repair, and expanding, over the old fort."

Arriving at the fort, they saw a small party of Indians walk in the open east gate. They carried dried strips of dark-fleshed fish. "They are trading salmon for other goods," Denis explained. He dismounted.

The men all dismounted. Denis looked them over, "It will be best if only Travis and I go in to make our inquiries. The rest of you wait here."

Having grown accustomed to following Denis' instructions, due to his knowledge of the country, they agreed. Denis looked at them, "Watch for those agents, in case they are still here."

Travis looked at Denis, his manner had changed. For his talk of hating Hudson's Bay, and avoiding them, he seemed comfortable here. He didn't act like a man who had been cheated by them, and was leery of being arrested for having torn up his license. Over the past several days, he was a typical French trapper in speech and habit, now he was sounding, and acting, more official. Something was suddenly different here, and different bothered him. He followed Denis into the fort through the east gate.

Two men met them inside. "I want to see Master McGillivray," Denis said to them.

Both men looked surprised. "Mr. Fournier! We did not

recognize you at first," one replied. "Master McGillivray is in his office."

Denis nodded, and walked on. Travis was eyeing him suspiciously as they walked. He was becoming uncomfortable with the turn of Denis' manner, and his familiarity of the fort. Those men knew him, and he obviously was on good terms with the Post Master. He didn't have his rifle, but he could fight his way out with the Bowie.

Denis glanced at Travis, taking in his concerned look, and steady eye contact. "You are not walking into a trap, I promise. I'll explain it to all of you once I have seen Master McGillivray."

"Yeah, you'd better," Travis replied.

The north and south walls of the compound were comprised of store rooms, trade store, barracks, and from the smells coming out, a kitchen. Denis walked to the northside, and knocked on a door.

The door was opened by a man, dark haired, clean shaven save for sideburns running to the turn of his jaws. He looked at the two, then smiled, "Mr. Fournier, you have returned. Come in."

Denis and Travis walked into the small office. Travis was silent, yet all of his senses and muscles were tensed for action.

Denis gestured to Travis, "This is Travis Walker. Travis, Master McGillivray."

McGillivray extended his hand to Travis, and they shook hands. McGillivray studied Travis, "You look rather confused, Mr. Walker. Did Mr. Fournier not explain himself to you?"

"Not completely, as I'm learnin'," Travis replied.

"Before we get into explanations," Denis said. "Booth, Carter, Holmes, and Phillips came back this way from the American rendezvous. They are with a man named Duncan Black, who is a murderer and thief. Did they come back in here?"

McGillivray shook his head, "I did not see them, but I do not see every trader who comes in."

"They had four horses of pelts to trade here. It had to be an exceptional number of pelts. Did you see that?"

"There was a man who came in with a huge quantity of peltries. He claimed to have traded for them with the Indians to the east. I had to approve the purchase because it was a large amount."

"Was he a Scotsman, with red beard and long red hair?" Travis asked.

McGillivray looked at Travis, "That does describe him, yes."

"Those are all stolen pelts," Travis said. "Black led a gang that murdered trappers, and stole the pelts. He met with your agents at Pierre's Hole, and they were bringing the pelts here. Black's gang also murdered a woman, and two children, in St. Charles. We have been after them since then."

"Can you prove the pelts were stolen?" McGillivray asked. "Be assured, Mr. Walker, I am not doubting your account, however, if you can prove the peltries are stolen, it will strength the case against them."

"I might be able to, can I see them?"

"Yes, of course," McGillivray said. He led them out of the office to the storage room. Opening the door, the sunlight illuminated the room. He lit a lantern to shed more light over the stacked pelts. "That stack there is what your man brought in," McGillivray said pointing to a table covered with hundreds of dried pelts. "As you can see, it is a goodly lot."

Travis knew the only way he could prove the pelts were stolen was to find the muskrat pelts skinned and dried in Warren Gentry's fashion. He began to pull all the muskrat pelts from the pile. "One of the murdered trappers, whose pelts were stolen, skinned, and dried, his muskrat pelts in a way different from the normal way," Travis began. "I know his work. The dried pelt will have an inch or two of belly fur on the back side, and awl holes where he tied the bottom of the pelt down, squared-off, to a bar across the bottom of the willow frame."

Denis began to help Travis separate the muskrat pelts from the pile. Picking one up, he looked at it, flipped it around, then held it in the light, and looked at the fur on the inside. "Like this one?" he asked Travis.

Travis took it from him, "Yeah! That's his work. See the belly fur on the back, the awl holes, and square bottom?"

McGillivray nodded, "As you described it."

Denis helped Travis sort through the pelts. They pulled

a dozen muskrat pelts matching Gentry's style. "Here's your proof," Travis said to McGillivray.

"Good enough for me," McGillivray said. He looked at Denis, "The rogue agents must have waited outside while Black sold the peltries. They knew I would recognize them. They should still be close. Do you have the warrants on you?"

"I have them," Denis said.

"Give them to me, I will arrange their transport down river when you bring them to me," McGillivray said.

Denis took a folder from the inside pocket of his shirt, and handed it to McGillivray. "I kept them on me at all times. I didn't want to keep them in my pack, or saddlebag in the event I lost the horse."

"Good. Now, go bring them in."

Denis looked at Travis, "Come on, our hunt isn't over."

Denis walked at a quick pace out of the fort, with Travis beside him. When they got to the waiting group, Travis grabbed Denis by his upper arm and pulled him to a stop. "Alright, *Mister* Fournier, what's goin' on?"

Denis calmly removed Travis' hand from his arm, "Easy, Travis, I'm on your side."

The others were looking at the two of them, their expressions showing confusion, and concern. "What happened?" Nick asked.

"It seems Denis, and the Post Master, are old friends, and there's something goin' on between them in regards to the Bay agents."

"Do you want to catch up to Black, and the agents, or stand here and talk?" Denis asked.

"Stand here, and talk," Travis answered firmly. "Start talkin'."

"Okay, I'll explain quickly," Denis said. "We can get into details later, okay?"

"Depends on the quick explanation," Travis said.

"Headquarters for the Hudson's Bay Columbia District, of the Oregon Territory, is at Fort Vancouver, a couple hundred miles down the Columbia. The Chief Factor is, John McLoughlin. He's an excellent administrator, stern, but fair. His superiors want him to refuse aid to anyone who is not with the Bay, McLoughlin doesn't see it that way. The Governor of Hudson's Bay Company is George Simpson, he's the one who ordered the destruction of the beaver, and all fur, to keep the Americans back.

"That policy has been destructive to the Hudson's Bay's trappers who are fleeing to the American side to trap, and receive fair trade for their pelts. It has also cost trade with the Indians, by angering them. The fur desert policy has destroyed the means for the Indians to trap fur, and trade it to the fort for other things they want. So, like the Cayuse that attacked us, the Indians have taken to stealing what they need because their means of trade is gone, thanks to George Simpson. Factor McLoughlin is angry over the policy, and has not approved any Hudson's Bay agents to run people out of the territory, as Simpson demands.

"Four agents, the ones you encountered, are Booth,

Carter, Holmes, and Phillips. They were instructed by
Simpson to remove, or arrest, everyone from the territory
that was not licensed by Hudson's Bay. The four went
rogue, and thinking they had complete power from the
governor, could do what they pleased. They began stealing
from trappers, extorting money, and robbing who they
pleased. They are suspected in two murders as well. Factor
McLoughlin wants them caught, and brought to Fort
Vancouver for trial."

"Are you a Hudson's Bay agent?" Nick asked Denis.

"I am a Hudson's Bay guide. I have led Hudson's Bay
exploration parties for years. I know all of this country,
from north to south, and into the Rocky Mountains. Factor
Mcloughlin sent a letter, along with four arrest warrants,
to Master McGillivray, for the rogue agents. He commis-
sioned me to track them down, and arrest them. He gave
me the task because I know the country so well, and he
knows I can be trusted to do it.

"I started asking questions and learned they had gone
east. I suspected they were going to the Pierre's Hole
rendezvous to steal. I was headed that way, when I met
Remi and Paul, and then you. When you told me about the
men you hunted, I knew they had come back this way, and
I had missed them."

"I find all that hard to believe," Martin said. "That a
Hudson's Bay Factor cares about what Hudson's Bay agents
do to people. My experience with Hudson's Bay, on the
Red River, is quite different from what you describe here."

"I agree with Martin," Nick said. "I was hunted by the Hudson's Bay agents all over Rupert's Land because I wanted to trap on my own, without their owning me. I saw them arrest innocent men for petty offences, and leave their wives and children destitute."

"We had similar experiences in the Newcastle District," Remi said. "That's why we headed into the states. Now, you want us to believe Hudson's Bay is not a pack of scoundrels? You will have to do much more to convince me of that."

"Simpson rules from Rupert's Land, and his policies don't rest well with the officials in the Oregon Territory, and Columbia District," Denis replied. "They have learned from the mistakes made in Rupert's Land, and want to avoid those, as they lead to problems, and loss of profits. You see what destruction Simpson has caused by forcing Rupert's Land policies on the Columbia District. He came here once, and by that passed down his decrees, then returned. The worst of which is the fur desert policy. He is a long way from here, and doesn't see the ruin he has caused, nor does he care. Factor McLoughlin has sole control over the governing of this territory, and he wants to avoid those mistakes, so he ignores Simpson at every chance. Violators of the law, like the rogue agents, will face his justice."

The group stood in silence considering what Denis had said. "Will we be arrested, or driven out, because we are not Hudson's Bay employees?" Nick asked.

Denis looked at him, "If you were going to be, do you think we would be standing here talking?"

Nick shrugged, "Maybe, no. Maybe, yes. This matter is not finished, yet."

Denis scowled at Nick, then looked at Travis, "Does that satisfy you?"

"Why didn't you tell us that right up front?" Travis asked.

"Because, I had no idea who you were. I wasn't going to divulge my mission to anyone I didn't know. Then, when you all starting talking about how you hated Hudson's Bay, the last thing I wanted you to know was why I was out there. You might have killed me, for all I know. Once I got you here, I could prove my intentions to find these men. As it turned out, I am able to help you find your man as well."

"What do you know about Duncan Black," Travis asked. "I don't see how Black could have known about the agents being at the rendezvous. How did they get together?"

"I know nothing of Duncan Black, but I can see no possible way he could have set this up with them in advance," Denis replied. "You said, Black, came from the east. I know for a fact, the agents I hunt, came from the west. I'm sure it was by pure chance they encountered each other."

"Here is what I think," Martin began. "Black heard that Bay agents were at the rendezvous, and he looked them up to learn where he could sell the stolen pelts. "Since they were all with Hudson's Bay, and he had four horses full of pelts, they invited him along. They did not care how he came by them, they just wanted in on the profit of the pelts."

Denis looked at Martin, "That would fit them, yes."

"They threw Luther Monk to us; I wonder if they will do the same with Black?" Nick asked.

"They will keep him in the party," Denis replied. "He's one of them."

"Where will they go from here?" Travis asked Denis.

"They won't go downriver, because that leads to Fort Vancouver," Denis answered. "Factor McLoughlin will have men watching for them. They know they are wanted, because they didn't go into the fort with Black when he sold the pelts. That means they know the Columbia District is dangerous for them."

"They will not go back to Rupert's Land because the governor told them to work over here," Martin said. "If they go back there, the governor will want to know why they left their assignment. That would put them in trouble."

"They have to go back to the American side, and lose themselves in the mountains," Denis said.

"And, keep killing and robbing," Travis remarked.

"If they are going to head back to the states, they'll follow the Snake around to stay with water, rather than go across the hot, dry country," Denis said. "That's what I would do, if I was going back."

"Are you goin' back?" Travis asked.

"I'm going wherever I have to in order to find them," Denis replied. "So, if you are all satisfied with my explanation, can we go after them?"

As one, the men nodded their heads. "I take it, you know this Snake River country?" Travis asked.

"I do," Denis answered.

"You have a problem killin' 'em if they put up a fight?" Travis asked.

"They won't fight, they'll run," Denis said.

"Maybe," Travis agreed. "We intend to kill Duncan Black; he's not runnin' anywhere."

"He's all yours," Denis said. "My job is to find the four agents."

Travis held his eyes on Denis for a moment, then took the roan's reins from Martin, "Lead on."

10

They rode north along the Columbia, headed for the mouth of the Snake River. Coming to a fish camp of Palouse Indians, they stopped and watched them for a moment. The women were busy filling drying racks with salmon and whitefish, the children had the duty of keeping the birds away from the meat. The men were still fishing, bringing in more fish to be dried.

"These are Palouse Indians," Denis said. "They come here from the mountains to collect fish for the winter. They'll be here until the end of summer, then head back with packs of fish." He moved his horse up to a drying rack where two boys stood by it with sage branches to chase off the birds. In Palouse, he asked the boys if they had seen five white men ride by, one with a big red beard.

The boys pointed up river, and answered in their native tongue.

Denis looked back at the group, "They passed by here yesterday, going toward the Snake. They had two pack horses."

"They did something with the other two horses," Travis remarked.

"Probably traded them to the fort," Denis replied.

"They must have stopped somewhere for two days," Martin said. "They should be farther ahead than one day."

"Trading that much fur isn't a fast thing," Denis said. "They likely got here late, and Black spent hours in the dealing. That would account for an extra day."

"Black's used to selling small amounts of fur, quickly," Nick said. "I'm sure he didn't like having it take a long time. He wanted to get done, and get out."

"Hudson's Bay is not a local fur buyer who quotes a price, and you're done," Denis replied. "They take their time, and then there's the trading for supplies. The Indians like to dicker, and the fort traders are used to operating slowly."

"Martin has a point," Travis said. "With the Cayuse costin' us two days, and the extra times we rested the horses, they should have been three or four days ahead of us, not one."

"They might have waited back a day, or two, making sure it was safe to go into the fort," Denis said.

"Why, would they?" Nick asked. "Did they know you

were after them, or they had arrest warrants? It seems they wouldn't have come back here, if they knew they were going to be arrested."

Denis paused a silent moment with a look of consternation on his face. "You are right. They would not have known about the warrants. That means, someone at the fort must have warned them, or they all would have gone right into the fort to trade. They were warned away by someone who is friendly with them, and that person had to be in the fort. I'll find out who that is."

Denis called to the boys again, and asked them if they had seen where the men were camped before they rode by.

The boys pointed to a stand of cedar trees on a hillside, and spoke a few words.

Denis looked back at the group, "The boys said they were camped for two days by those cedar trees."

"That would account for the extra days," Travis said. "They were hidin', until they felt safe, and even then, they sent Black in alone."

Denis nodded, "Yes, however, there was no reason for them to be scared, they thought they had all the power from the governor. Then, someone told them they were wanted by Factor McLoughlin, and they were scared to come in. Now, they have traded and left, so feel they are in the clear, and can escape. They are only one day from the fort, with their trade goods and money. Trade goods," he muttered, then looked back toward the fort. "I'll be right back, stay here."

"Now, what's he up to?" Nick asked out loud.

"He has been a mystery right from the start," Martin said. "I still am leery of anyone associated with Hudson's Bay, no matter what he claims."

"I'm going to follow him," Nick said, as he reined his horse around.

"If he's pullin' a trick on us," Travis called out to Nick, "shoot him."

Nick nodded his acknowledgement as he rode after Denis.

Denis rode to the fort and dismounted, tying his horse to a post, he walked in through the gate. Nick stopped fifty yards out, and waited.

A quarter hour passed before Denis walked out, and mounted his horse. Turning the horse, he saw Nick waiting for him. Riding up to Nick, he said, "Don't trust me, do you?"

Nick shrugged, "Old habits."

"What habits are those?"

"Never trust a river pirate, or a Hudson's Bay official."

"I'm not an official, I am a guide with a commission to perform a service to the law of the district, and I am a Frenchman. We are countrymen, would I betray a countryman?"

Nick raised one eyebrow at him, "You've never known a countryman to betray another? You must have spent your life under the covers of your bed."

"Maybe, it's because I never *would*," Denis replied, locking eyes with Nick.

Nick held his eyes for a long moment, then said, "You're angry at my slur against your honor."

"I take my word and honor seriously. Challenge them, and you challenge me."

Nick continued to hold eyes with Denis, then he grinned, "A man who values his honor, is a man who can be trusted. A man who will abide an insult to his word, or honor, is no man at all, nor one to be trusted. I was testing you."

"Did I pass the test, or should we fight?" Denis asked tersely.

"You have my trust, countryman. Besides, if we fought, I would kill you, and I have come to like you." Nick turned his horse, and rode back to the group.

Denis followed him. He understood how the men felt, he had in a way deceived them, but it was because he needed to prove his intentions were not to harm them. In all honesty, he understood their skepticism, Hudson's Bay had done little to make friends of the Rupert's Land inhabitants.

"What did you go back for?" Travis asked Denis.

"Two things," Denis replied. "I told Master McGillivray to find the man who warned the rogue agents. He said he would find the man, and arrest him as well. The other thing was, to learn what supplies Black purchased."

"What did you learn?" Travis asked.

"He took some in gold, some in supplies, and – a keg of rum."

A light of understanding came over Travis' face, as it did Nick's. "That is a lot of rum, and they would drink it all. I know Black is a heavy drinker, never one to pass up liquor," Nick said. "If they started on it last night, they will still be passed out."

"They've had a long trip with no liquor, and men like that will drink," Denis said. "That was the idea I had in going back to check. I believed they would take some liquor with them. I'll keep asking the Indian boys as we go, if they are camped, the boys will know where."

"That was a good hunch," Travis said.

"I have my moments," Denis said as he began riding, the others followed. Travis leaned toward Nick, "I trust him."

Nick nodded, "Me, too."

Nick looked back at the others, and pointed at Denis' back, and gave a nod of approval.

Remi, Paul, and Martin nodded back their acknowledgement.

Another thirty minutes brought them to a set of fish racks in a Wallawalla camp. Denis asked the boys if they had seen the men. Talking in their native tongue, they pointed at a grove of locust trees growing out of a tangle of small cedar trees, and brush.

"Do you know all the languages?" Travis asked Denis.

"Enough of each to get by," Denis replied. "That grove of locust trees, ahead. The boys said they saw those men set up their camp in there. They have not seen them come out."

"Sleeping off the rum," Travis remarked.

"I hope so."

Travis chuckled, "Those boys don't miss much, do they?"

"They have a boring job for active boys, but if they fail to do their jobs, the fish will be lost to the birds, and they will be punished," Denis explained. "That doesn't stop their eyes from watching everything going on around them."

They rode toward the trees.

A thin tendril of smoke rose up from the behind the brush. The men separated, and encircled the campsite. Pinning it against the brush barrier. The last of the fire's smoke spun in the breeze, the empty rum cask lay on the ground, along with five metal cups.

They sat on their horses, looking down on the five men snoring under their blankets. Duncan Black's tangle of red hair and beard showed above his point blanket.

"That's Black," Nick said.

"And, the rogue agents," Denis said. Dismounting, he pulled his rifle from the scabbard. Nick dismounted as well. The other men pulled their rifles, but remained mounted looking down on the sleeping outlaws.

Nick pulled his Bowie, and hunkered down at the top of Black's head. He began to tap the flat of the blade against Black's head. After the fifth tap, Black snorted, and swiped at his head. Nick then smacked the blade down hard on Black's head.

Black let out a howl of pain, and a curse. Sitting up, he grumbled as he rubbed the spot of the blow. His eyes were slits as he tried to look around through the blinding headache brought on by the rum's hangover.

Suddenly, sensing someone was behind him, he rolled over, and leaning on his left elbow, stared at Nick. His brain taking several seconds to comprehend who he was looking at. At the realization of who it was, he asked in a hoarse voice, "Nick? What are you doing here?"

Martin stepped up beside Nick, who was still hunkered down, the knife in his hand. "Remember me?" Martin snarled. Then, he kicked Black in the face.

Black let out a cry of pain, as he fell over backwards. With his hands clamped over his face, he let out a spew of curses. His commotion woke the other men. They sat up looking around, their bloodshot eyes showing the effects of the rum. They looked up at the mounted men, then to Denis, who stood in front of them, his rifle aimed at them.

"What is this!" one demanded.

Travis dismounted, and walked up to the Bay agent. "You said, you would see me again. Looks like you were right."

The agent's mind cleared as he recognized Travis. "You! I will have you arrested for this! I am a Hudson's Bay official!"

"You are the one under arrest, Mr. Booth," Denis said.

Booth glowered at Denis, "Who in the blazes are you?"

"I've been sent by Factor McLoughlin to arrest you, and bring you to trail in Fort Vancouver," Denis replied.

Denis' statement struck Booth, his sudden expression revealed that he had known he was to be arrested, but he attempted to counter it. "We work for Governor Simpson, and he will have your head for this!"

Travis stepped forward and kicked Booth solidly in the ribs. With a cry of pain, he gripped his chest. "Shut up!" Travis snapped. "I'm sick of listenin' to your noise. You helped two murderers escape. We got both, and now we have you. Say another word, and I'll kick out another rib."

The other three outlaw agents sat still and quiet.

Black took his hands down from his face and stared at Martin. A bleeding cut, and a darkening bruise showed under his left eye.

"We have been following you since you murdered my family in St. Charles," Martin said in a low, hard voice. "You are the last one we need to kill."

Black held one hand up, "Wait a minute, I had no part in that. That was all Antoine. He did that."

Nick stood up, rolling the Bowie in his hand, and looking at Black. "You and Antoine tried to pin it on me by planting the jewelry in my pocket. I told Antoine, and you, to stay away from Martin's family. You didn't listen, now you'll die, like the rest of the gang."

"Now, wait Nick, we're old friends . . ."

"I'm not your friend, never was," Nick replied icily.

"Find Antoine," Black stammered out. "Make him tell you it was him, not me."

"I know it was you," Nick said. "I know it was Antoine, too. He never caught up with you because I gutted him."

Black's eyes widened with fear. He looked at Martin, who held a glare on him. "We can work something out. I'll give you money."

In a snarl of rage, Martin rushed in and began to drive bone-cracking kicks into Black's body. Black cried out, shrieking in panic. *"Did my children scream in fear when you raped them, and cut their throats!"* Martin screamed at him as he drove in one brutal kick after another. *"Did they! Curse you to hell – did they! You dare to offer me money for the lives of my children! Curse you!"* Martin continued to kick him until Black could only lay on the ground and whimper.

Tears poured down Martin's face as all the pain and rage was poured out on the man who had led the attack on his loved ones. Nick finally put his hand on Martin's shuddering shoulder. "Easy, Martin, leave something for us to hang."

Martin stopped, his breath coming in heaving sobs.

"It's okay, Martin," Nick said in a soft voice, "we got the scoundrel. He won't leave this place."

Martin backed up, weeping.

The Bay men stared, transfixed in shock at Martin's furious attack.

"He, and his gang, raped and cut the throats of that man's wife, and young daughters," Travis said to them.

"That's the man you protected. If it was up to me, I'd just shoot you, and leave you here to rot, but Mr. Fournier has a job to do. You'd better cooperate with him, or by-God, I will shoot the lot of you."

The Bay men remained silent.

"Get up!" Denis commanded them.

The three men stood up. Remi and Paul had dismounted, but stood in place, taken aback by Martin's frightening outburst. At hearing Denis' order to the prisoners, Remi snapped out of his stupor, and pulled leather thongs from his saddlebag. He, and Paul, tied the Bay men's hands behind them.

Travis looked down at Booth, "Get up. You ain't hurt that bad."

"I'm injured," Booth said in a low voice. "You broke a rib."

"I'll break a couple more if you don't get up."

"I cannot," Booth snapped.

Travis looked at Denis, "Go ahead and take those three, I'm putting a ball in this one's head, and leave him here."

"He *is* resisting," Denis said. "I'll tell Master McGillivray he pulled a weapon, and we had to shoot him." He mounted his horse, then looked at the bound prisoners. "Start walking."

"Why can't we ride?" Carter asked.

"Because you will be going to Fort Vancouver by boat, you won't need horses. Now, start walking!"

"We will come with you," Remi said. "It will be easier if

three of us take them." Remi looked at Travis, "We want to go back with you. Will you meet us at the fort?"

Travis nodded, "We'll pick you up there." He then pulled a rifle from the scabbard, and walked up to Booth as he thumbed back the hammer and set a cap on the nipple.

Booth's eyes bulged in terror, "You are really going to shoot me?"

"Yeah, I've got no use for you. Shootin' you's no different to me then shootin' a thievin' coyote."

"Don't shoot me, I will go with them." He got to his feet and walked haltingly after Denis.

"Denis," Travis called out. "You have another one. He was miraculously healed."

Paul dismounted. He tied Booth's hands behind his back, and joined him with the others.

Travis and Nick stood over Black. Martin had regained his composure, and joined them.

Black lay rolling back and forth on the ground, moaning in pain, and whimpering.

"Get a rope out of the pack," Travis said to Nick. He grabbed Black by the hair and forced him to sit up. His face was battered and bleeding. "We're goin' to hang you, you lousy cur."

Black whimper, and tried to beg, but his battered lips formed no words.

"You'll find no sympathy here," Travis said to him. He looked up at the trees, "I don't see a good hangin' branch, but we can run the rope over that fork right there, and pull him up."

Nick looked up into a tree, and tossed the end of the rope over the fork ten feet above his head, and kept flipping the rope until the end came down. He tied a noose in the end.

Martin and Travis dragged the blubbering man over to the tree. Nick put the noose over his neck and tightened it. Black was openly bawling as Travis and Martin roughly pulled him to his feet while Nick caught up the slack against Black's neck. They all took hold of the rope, and pulled Black off the ground, then secured the end of the rope to the trunk of a small cedar.

Taking a piece of tanned elk hide from his pack, Travis took a piece of charred wood from the fire and wrote on it, *child rapist and murderer.* Black's body had stopped struggling as Travis hung the sign around his neck.

Releasing the outlaws' horses from the picket line, they turned them loose.

"I don't like this country much," Travis said. Let's pick up Remi and Paul, and go back to the Rockies."

They mounted their horses and left the scene.

They caught up with Denis, Remi, and Paul and rode along with them. Martin rode in silence.

The Indians at the fish camps stared as they rode by, pushing the bound prisoners ahead of them.

Reaching the fort, Denis, Remi, and Paul dismounted and escorted the prisoners inside.

Travis, Martin, and Nick waited outside for them to come back out. A half-hour passed before Remi and Paul walked out, and mounted their horses. They rode back to the others.

Denis came walking out of the fort toward them. They moved the horses to meet him.

Denis looked up at them, "I take it Duncan Black has been dealt with?"

"He has," Travis replied. "McGillivray happy with his prisoners?"

"He is, and he found the man who warned them. He's going along to see Factor McLoughlin, and that will not be a nice meeting for him. I, and two other men, will be taking the prisoners in the morning, bound for Fort Vancouver. It's been a pleasure gentleman." He extended his hand up to Travis, who took it in his big hand. "Anytime you decide to come back to the Rockies, you can find us at a rendezvous."

"I might head that way one day," Denis replied. He looked up at Martin, seeing the strain, and pain in his eyes. "It is not easy to lose the ones you love; I know that by experience. I pray that you will find peace, and a way to let the past go."

Martin shook his hand, "Thank you. Perhaps, one day."

Denis looked up at Nick, closing one eye he studied him, "So, I passed the test, did I?"

Nick grinned, "You did." He extended his hand, and they shook.

Denis pointed at the Snake River, "Follow it all the way

back. The first hundred miles is barren, but then it starts to get into the mountains. After a few days you will begin to recognize your country."

"You take care, now," Travis said to him.

"What is it, the trappers say in the Rocky Mountains? Watch your topknot?" Denis asked.

Travis grinned, "Watch your'n." He led them to the north to find the Snake River.

11

The sun was setting in a brilliant display of orange, red, and blue, as the men led the horses to drink from the Henry's Fork. Men and horses were bone-weary, and exhausted. It had been weeks of relentless pursuit of Duncan Black's gang. Months since Martin and Nick had left St. Charles. They all stood in their own thoughts as the horses drank.

Leading the horses from the water, they staked them out on the grass. Martin had spoken little over the days since they left Duncan Black hanging from a tree with his crimes hung around his neck. The journey had been a life-changing experience for them all. Nick, finally able to reveal his long-held secrets. Travis, coming to grips with his pain, and loss, and the importance of returning to the world, and his friends. Hiding from the world had changed nothing, his boys were still gone.

For Martin, the questions, doubts, and fears lingered. He still wrestled with his pain, and the unknown future before him. The guilty had paid, but it had not brought his wife and children out of their graves. His life had not returned to the days when they laughed together, and Sharice brought him treats from the city. Nothing had changed, so where did he go from here?

Remi and Paul were wise enough to sense their new friends were dealing with problems, and did not pry. They did all they could to help, but without interference. Nick had privately told them about Martin's ordeal, and why they had come west. The two, along with Travis, went to work setting up the camp.

Martin wandered a short way downstream, and sat down on a log that paralleled the river. He stared out at the river, watching the current pass by like it had for a thousand years. At one time, he had a successful business, and a wonderful wife, and loving daughters. He had offered his labors for them, and poured out his love on them. He lived for Colette, Sharice and Yvonne.

Then, in one horrifying hour, it was all snatched from him, leaving him in inconsolable agony. Then, he lived to deliver retribution on their murderers, and as he had poured out his love on his family, he now poured out his wrath on the wretched filth who had destroyed them. Now, what did he live for? What was left?

Nick came walking slowly downstream. He knew his friend was struggling with his thoughts, and what to do next. He had felt that way when his mother died, and he was taken by Antoine. The first time Antoine beat him, he knew his life was forever changed. He had struggled with what he should do. Run away, or stay where he had some manner of security, even if it was as a battered child being indoctrinated into a life of crime. He had resolved to become stronger than what opposed him, and had lost his soul in the process. Then, he recovered his soul, defied them all, and blazed his own trail. Martin would have to do the same, or end up like Travis had been, locked away inside himself, never living, never breathing a free breath that the past did not own.

Nick stepped up next to him, "Mind some company?"

Martin looked up at him, "I could use some company right now."

Nick sat down. He looked out at the river, "I like this country a lot better than that dry, land on the Columbia."

"Yes, I do as well," Martin replied.

"There was a time when my life was like that dry, barren country," Nick began. "I was trapped in a bad situation. Orphaned, my parents who I loved, gone. I told you that my father broke through the ice, and drowned. I never told you the misery I went through after that. When he went under, I was completely unable to help him. I had shoved my arm into the freezing water, hoping he would see it and grab ahold, but he never did. I relived that moment, those few seconds, a hundred-years-worth of seconds. I heard that crack, the splash, my father's cry of surprise, in my every waking hour, and countless sleepless nights. If I had done this, or if I had done that, if I had been faster, I could have saved him. If we had not taken the path across the lake, the ice never would have broken. If – if – if, my life was a nightmare of if's."

Martin looked at him, "But, you could have done nothing. Once a man goes through the ice in a deep lake, it is rare for him to come back out the same hole. It was not your fault."

"Try telling my twelve-year-old mind that. I couldn't let it go. I was always thinking of ways I could have made it different."

"You did all you could," Martin said. "You could not have made a different."

Nick looked Martin in the eyes, "No, I couldn't, and neither could you."

Martin showed confusion, "What do you mean?"

"If I had fought harder. If I had two guns. If I had not been so weak to let the punches knock me out. If I never let Duncan Black in my shop. If Colette had not come downstairs at that moment. If I had never taken them to St. Charles." Nick held his friend's eyes, "If."

Martin stared at Nick, "How did you know that was in my mind?"

"Because, it was in mine. I know the look. I know you Martin, you are a courageous man, I know you fought as hard as you could, but against ten men, you had no chance. You had no idea who Duncan Black was when he came in your shop, you could not have prevented that. Blaming yourself, will not change what could not have been changed. I didn't bring my father back by it."

Martin looked out to the river, "I know, but how do I make it stop."

"Do you want it to stop?" Nick asked.

Martin turned his eyes back to Nick, "What do you mean?"

"Sometimes, a man doesn't want it to stop. He feels he must relive it over and again. Maybe, it's because he is afraid if he doesn't relive it, the ones he lost will fade from his mind. Maybe, it's because he feels he made mistakes that cost him the ones he loved, like Travis did. Look at Travis, for two years he relived the loss of his sons, he wouldn't let it go. He blamed himself for a decision he made. Every day he told himself of his guilt. He was holed up in a rotting house in fear of living again. "That's what I mean."

Martin stared at him, but did not reply.

"Do you want to relive it every day, press the guilt on yourself forever, or put it to rest? Lay it down, but keep the good memories, or let, 'if', rule the rest of your life? Stop blaming yourself, or you will end up in some rotting house, dying by inches."

"I miss them, so much," Martin whispered as tears ran down his cheeks.

"Yes, you do, and it is good to grieve, however, after you have grieved, you must move on."

"How, do I let them go?"

"You don't let them go, you take them with you, but, let them lie in peace."

Martin sniffed, and ran his hand across his face, wiping the tears away. "I have such great darkness overshadowing me. How did you overcome that?"

"When my mother died, I was fourteen, wondering what my future held. All I could see was darkness, and fear. Then, Antoine took me, and I learned what darkness and fear really was."

"You overcame it, though," Martin said in a low voice.

"Yes, but I took the wrong path at first. I filled my veins with iron, my mind with strength that refused all fear. The pain of losing my parents, I pushed to the back of my mind. The physical pain of Antoine's beatings, and those of the pirates, put iron in my spine. That was the strength I needed at the time, until that day I told you about, when I saw the portrait of, 'my beloved ladies'. We had killed their husband and father. It shook my world like a keg of gunpowder going off under my feet. I knew then, my idea of strength was not strength, but the false strength of a bully, and that was not the strength of a real man.

"I walked away from them, and that evil life, but my guilt sunk me into dark despair. I had shamed my father, mother, and myself. The darkness was the blackest of nights. I disappeared into the woods, and spent countless hours in contemplation, thinking of what my father stood for, and what he believed, and that's when I realized what real strength was. To stand up for the weak, not abuse them, was what a real man did. That was my father, and I could still change, and be a man he would be proud to call his son. I left the guilt behind, determined to be a better man, and the darkness faded away.

"Your experiences over these last months have put iron in your blood and spine. You stood up and fought for the weak, for Colette, and your children. You did what a real man is supposed to do. You were beaten down, but not from cowardice, but by being outnumbered. You have the real strength to overcome your fear and guilt, not to be owned by it. You just have to use it. That is how you overcome the darkness."

Martin stared at Nick as he considered what he had said. "To be my own man, and not owned by my fears and guilt, you mean? To accept that I did all I could, and did not let them down?"

Nick nodded, "Yes."

Martin looked out at the river for a full minute, then let out a shaky breath, "The darkness is my guilt, isn't it?"

"Yes, that is the darkness. Remove the guilt, and in time, the darkness will lift."

"I can do that. I will take them with me in my heart, but let them lie in peace. Constantly stirring up that night serves no good for them, or me. I did all I could. I did not cower, or shirk my duty to them."

"That's right, not by one ounce did cower, or shirk your duty."

Martin drew in a deep breath and let it out. "I am not sure what to do next. I feel that I should go back, and take up my business again, and tend to their graves."

"Tending to the graves is a noble thing, but how long will that sustain you? Do you have friends to talk to when you are troubled? People who care if you live or die?"

Martin was silent for a long moment, then asked, "Are you going back?"

"No. I have nothing there."

"Then, the answer to your question, is, no. You would be my only friend, and if you stay here, I would have no friends."

"I have learned that friends are a fleeting thing. It's amazing how quickly they desert you when they find that you are down on your luck, or need a sympathetic ear. I had no friends, except you, until I came out here. Now, I have many friends, and so have you. Men, who only care about your mettle, and character, not how much gold is in your purse. Men who will listen when you need to talk. Men, who will stand by you, and fight to the death, because you are their friend. Like the men did to rescue Willy and Aaron from the Blackfeet. You won't find that back in St. Charles."

Martin shook his head, "No, I would not." He smiled, "Like Enoch, Coon Eyes Charlie, Bullfrog, Bearbait Jimmy,

Nels. Characters, the lot of them, but good men, better than I have ever known, except for you."

"There's Travis as well. You gave him a reason to live again, and he is better for it," Nick said.

Martin nodded, "He is the best of men."

"Yes, he is. More importantly, he's our friend."

"Yes. He went the full way to help us. He did not have to do that."

"That's what mountain men do, and I want to remain with them."

"I do as well."

Nick put his hand on Martin's shoulder, "I smell coffee – mountain man coffee."

Martin smiled, "I hope Paul did not make it."

Nick stood up, and laughed, "He needs to learn to make it properly. I dropped some on a rock, and the rock didn't melt. Travis' coffee will melt a rifle barrel. That's how it's supposed to be made."

Martin stood up, "He will learn." He looked at Nick, "Thank you for going all this way with me."

"I'm your friend, Martin, would you expect less?"

Martin shook his head, "No, not from a mountain man."

It was mid-day when they rode into Pierre's Hole. The valley was quiet. No raucous shouting, gunfire, or racing horses. The line of tepees along the creek were gone. The camps struck, and everyone gone, except for the smoke coming from a fire on Teton Creek. Travis led them toward it.

Staked out on the grass were fourteen horses. Sitting around the fire with coffee cups in their hands, and pipes in their mouths, were, Coon Eyes Charlie, Bullfrog, Hugo, Enoch, Aaron, Stinker Willy, Bearbait Jimmy, and Nels. They calmly watched Travis' party as they rode up.

Travis pulled the roan to a stop and grinned at them, "Didn't anyone tell you rendezvous was over?"

Charlie took the pipe from his mouth, and feigned a look around, "Whal, call me a greenhorn pilgrim, when did ever'one leave?"

"I told yuh they was all headin' out, yuh thick-headed Injun fighter," Stinker said, "but yuh don't listen to no one."

Travis laughed, "Okay, smart boys."

"Did yuh git 'em?" Bullfrog croaked.

"We got 'em," Travis replied.

"Monk, too?" Hugo asked.

"He's hangin' from a tree back on Henry's Fork," Travis answered.

Hugo tapped his pipe as he nodded, "Good. Rifle ball's too good fer the likes o' that belly-crawlin' snake."

"How come you boys are still here?" Travis asked.

"Waitin' on you," Charlie replied. "About time yuh got back."

"Why?" Travis asked.

Hugo snorted, and jabbed his pipe stem at Travis, "Will

yuh listen to him? *Why.* Cuz yer our friend yuh bonehead, that's why. If yuh didn't come back purt-soon, we was gonna go lookin' fer yuh."

"Well," I surely do appreciate it," Travis said.

The men looked over the party. "Appears yuh all come back in one piece, and even picked up a couple strays along the way," Enoch said.

"This is Remi and Paul," Travis said. He looked at the two, "You'll get to know all these rascals in time."

"Well, now that yer finally back," Nels said, "Jimmy, and me, can head back fer the Poudre. Figured to save you the trip down thar to git yer gear and horse."

"Thanks," Travis said. "You headin' back now?"

"Yup," Nels said. He stood up, tapped out his pipe, and put it in his possibles pouch. "Wasted 'nough time on yuh, Big Walker. Come on, Jimmy, we's burnin' daylight."

Jimmy and Nels looked up at Travis. "Don't be a stranger, come on down and visit," Nels said.

"We'll do that," Travis replied.

Nels helped lead Jimmy out to the horses.

"Jimmy's gettin' worse," Charlie said.

"Good thing he's got Nels," Travis remarked.

"He'll always have one of us," Charlie said as he stood up.

Nick gave Martin a knowing glance.

Martin nodded, "Mountain men."

"Where yuh figgerin' to summer, Big Walker?" Enoch asked. "Need to make plans for trappin' season."

Travis looked at the men with him. "Where do you want to go?"

"You were going to show us Colter's hell," Martin said. "How about there?"

Travis smiled at Martin, "You're stayin' then?"

Martin smiled, "I'm in the best of company here."

Travis held his eyes on Martin, "Yeah, you are, none better." He studied Martin for a few silent seconds, then asked, "You goin' to be okay?"

Martin nodded, "Yes. I am sure there will be rough days, but I have friends to help me through it."

"That you do," Travis replied.

Martin looked at Travis, "How about you? Are you going to be okay?"

Travis nodded, "Yeah, I'm goin' to be okay. I can let the boys rest in peace."

"You have friends here," Martin said.

Charlie walked up to Travis, "Yuh plan on plaverin' all day, or give us a hand with the packs?"

Travis looked at Martin and grinned, "Except, I might shoot Charlie."

"Yeah, yeah, talk's cheaper'n than Sublette's whiskey," Charlie said. "You ain't shootin' nobody." He looked at Martin, grinned, and winked, "It's good to have him back, but don't tell him that, or his head'll swell up like a bloated buffalo."

"I heard that," Travis said.

Charlie looked up at Travis, "You didn't hear nothin'.

We ain't never gettin' to the Yellerstone if you jist sit thar jackin' yer jaws. Come on." Charlie walked off toward the horses.

Martin laughed, "The best of men."

Travis shook his head and smiled, "Yeah. He's right though, we ain't gettin' to the Yellowstone sittin' here." He stepped off the roan."

Martin dismounted, and walked beside Travis. "Boiling mud, and smoking rivers, huh?"

"And, water that shoots a thousand feet in the air!" Travis replied.

Martin grinned, "This I have to see."

Travis slapped Martin on the back, "You will. You will."

HISTORICAL NOTE

The Route

The era of the mountain man was distinctive in character and exploration, a time never to be repeated. In 1832, the year of this story, there were no towns between the western Missouri border and the Pacific Coast. There were no settlements, or forts, except those of Hudson's Bay in the Oregon Territory. Fort Laramie and Fort Hall had yet to be built. The first missionaries, and wagon trains were still years away. This is how it has to be told, or it runs the risk of becoming a bit of Hollywood nonsense.

In the, *Return of Travis Walker*, I take you on a journey across a country that was roughly mapped, but not to the detail it is today. The many creeks, passes, and camps were known by their trapper names, and how to get there was orally passed on, yet not always accurately. As Travis found out when he was told the Teton River flowed into the Snake, only to learn it actually flowed into Henry's Fork.

Call this trilogy, a geography and history lesson, with a little adventure mixed in for flavor. Should you look up old maps of the era, as I used for accuracy, you will find the names of the places and streams marked on them. The rivers, and streams, served as map lines as they always led to some point, or landmark, and not like wandering across the plains, or desert, wondering where you were going. Today, some of those names have been changed, or new flood control reservoirs have covered the streams and landmarks.

The journey of Martin and Prisque (Nick), once out of St. Charles, follows the road to Columbia, Missouri. Then, on the trail to Fort Osage, where they find Travis who had hidden himself from the world. Fort Osage was built by William Clark in 1812, to trade with the Osage Indians. The fort was abandoned in 1822. The trail passing the ruins is where the historic Santa Fe Trail began.

Here, Travis joins them to begin his own rebuilding. They follow the Missouri River north to the mouth of the North Platte River. Today, that is just below, Omaha, Nebraska. The route along the North Platte takes them to present day, North Platte, Nebraska. They split off onto the South Platte River, through today's town of Julesburg, Colorado, to the mouth of the Cache La Poudre River.

Here they follow the Poudre (which is called 'Poo-der' today), through present day Fort Collins, Colorado.

They followed the Poudre River into the canyon, to the narrows, that now has Hwy 14 squeezed in between the roaring whitewater, and the mountainside. Coming around the narrows, they drop down into the beautiful Cache la Poudre valley. Climbing up the timbered mountains, through present day Virginia Dale, Colorado, they break onto the Laramie plains near present day Laramie, Wyoming. They crossed the Sweetwater River near Independence Rock.

The Green River they followed to the north is now partially under Flaming Gorge and Fontenelle reservoirs. They camp at present day, Daniel, Wyoming, then go over the pass along the Hoback River, that is now Hwy 191. Through Bondurant, known as Jackson's Little Hole, and connecting to the Snake River at present day Hoback Junction.

North along the Snake River to Jackson's Hole, present day Jackson, Wyoming. Then, west over Teton Pass, Hwy 22, coming out in the Teton Valley south of Victor, Idaho. Here was the Pierre's Hole rendezvous, centered around Driggs, Idaho. The Northwest Fur Company had set up where Hwy 33 crosses Teton Creek, on the south end of Driggs. The Flathead and Nez Perce encampments ran along Darby Creek, from present day Darby to Tetonia.

They next followed the Teton River to its mouth at Henry's Fork, located just north of County Road 2000 W, and north of Hinckley, Idaho. Traveling down the Henry's Fork to its mouth at the Snake River, west of the present day Menan Bridge, north of Menan, Idaho. The route they used along the Snake is Hwy 84, through Burley, Idaho, and on to Twin Falls, Idaho. The land at the time was desolate, arid, no water, no shade, and still, full of rattlesnakes. Today, it is productive farmland.

The canyon they encountered is the Snake River Canyon that begins east of Twin Falls. The bridge going over the canyon, into Twin Falls, gives you a spectacular view of the depth and length of the canyon. The little lake they found became known as, Vineyard Lake, and was a popular destination for Twin Falls residents. Access to the lake has recently been closed.

They get past the canyon, and back to the river where they meet Remi, Paul, and Denis. Denis describes the route to Fort Nex Perce, referencing *Riviere Aux Malad*, as a land mark. The river today is the Malad River, located north of Hagerman, Idaho. It is a short 2.5 mile long, spring-fed stream, used primarily for irrigation. It became known as the 'Sickly River' when a French trapper ate beaver meat caught on the river, and became very sick. It was attributed to the beaver feeding on poisonous roots, rendering the meat poison. The warning was passed on, and the stream was avoided.

They make their crossing of the Snake at a narrowing of the river between Bliss and Glenns Ferry. One of the few narrow places on the Snake River.

Going north, they break off from the Snake River at the Malheur River, at present day, Payette, Idaho, and follow Hwy 84, which traces the 'Old Immigrant Road/Old Oregon Trail', toward Baker City, Oregon. The place they camped is where, Hwy 84 and the Snake River, make a short connection south of Huntington, Oregon. The Snake, once again, curves back away from the highway. From here, they proceed up through the foothills of the Blue Mountains, and the present town of Baker City, Oregon. Continuing north, they begin the pass through the timbered higher elevations of the Blues. Their two-day camp was on the Grande Ronde River, just north of LaGrande, Oregon.

Topping out of the pass on what is now, 'Deadman's Pass', they begin the descent. The timbered mountains falling behind them, as they enter more barren, rolling hills, toward Pendleton, Oregon. The place they camped by a little creek, and could see the Umatilla River's treeline (Umatallow on the old maps), is near St. Andrew's Mission (est. 1847), south of Pendleton.

They crossed the Umatilla River at a wide southern-bend in the Mission, Oregon area. On the north side of the river, to the east, just past the Umatilla railroad bridge, is where they had the fight with the Cayuse. Leaving in the night, they set off to the northwest, along the current Cold Springs Road, tapping into Hwy 37, circumventing the rugged buttes, and coming to the Columbia River through the gently rolling hills. They reach the Columbia River fifteen miles downstream of Wallula Junction, Washington, which is six miles below Fort Nez Perce located on the Columbia at present day Wallula, Washington.

The final confrontation location, where the rogue agents are arrested and Duncan Black meets his demise is upriver from Wallula, at Two Rivers, Washington.

They return by way of the Snake River, and back into Pierre's Hole, where they started.

BONUS FEATURE

A Cost Beyond Measure

Prelude to the 'Return of Travis Walker' trilogy

Travis Walker stood at the edge of the Yellowstone River, where it ran into the lake. The wind still blew cold off the ice-covered water, but the April sun, shining out of a flawless blue sky, was warming the earth. The shorelines were still in ice, but the middle of the river, the deepest part, was breaking up.

Travis' twin sons, Alan and George walked up to him, and stood. "Ice is goin' out, Pa," Alan said. "Time to start some spring trappin', I'd say."

"Everyone's startin' to get restless," George remarked. "Figure it's time to break winter camp?"

Travis nodded, "Yeah. Just tryin' to decide where we should go."

"I like the Green," Alan put in. "Plenty of beaver."

"All the company trappers are on the Green now,"

George countered. "We need a place where they haven't run over it like a darn avalanche."

"George is right," Travis agreed. "Green's over-trapped now with the company trappers stoppin' there first off."

"We could head up the Yellowstone, and trap Blackfoot country," Alan said with a wry grin.

Travis raised an eyebrow as he looked at him. Alan was always in good humor. "Have a nice time. See you in the afterlife."

"Oh, come on, Pa, the Blackfeet are a kind and charitable people, always willin' to share, and be loving," Alan added with his grin widening.

"Down-right, cuddly, like a soft blanket," George added.

Travis snorted, "Sure, if you consider a nest of rattlesnakes, cuddly. I think we'll stay a little more to the south, thank you very much."

"Speakin' of snakes, how about the Snake?" George suggested. "Lot's of side streams, I don't think the company trappers have even been on it.

Travis began to slowly nod, "Yeah, down from Jackson's Hole, maybe where the Hoback comes in. What do you boys think about that?"

"Yup," George said.

Alan nodded, "Let's go. Winter camps breakin' up. All the other men are ready to go, and I'm anxious to be off and doin'!"

"Let's go back and see what everyone's plannin'," Travis said. They turned and walked back to the camp.

Fourteen trappers, all friends, had put in together to spend the winter along the Indian-free Yellowstone River, by the lake where Indians refused to go because of evil spirits. They had set up their shelters in the lodgepole stands, and grazed their horses in the grass along the river. The winter had been kind to them, and only a couple feet of snow had been on the ground at any one time. The tough mountain horses had been able to paw through it, and eat.

Travis and the boys walked back into the camp that was spread out through hundreds of feet of lodgepole pine. Smoke from the fires rose up into the air, portions of deer and elk carcasses hung from the trees. Piles of fall-caught pelts were wrapped in tarps for protection from the elements.

"We're ready to head out for spring trappin'," Travis announced to the group.

The men began to gather around Travis and the boys. They all had their partners from the fall, and years before. "I think we're all ready to break camp," Enoch Rose agreed.

"Big Walker, where you and the boys figurin' to go?" Coon Eyes Charlie asked.

"Oh, that's a big secret," Alan replied with his usual grin.

Charlie looked at him, as he fought back a grin. Everyone liked the Walker boys, especially Alan, as he was always coming up with something funny to say. "Fine, be like that. See if I ever tell you anythin' again. I won't tell yuh my big secret, now."

"What is it?" Alan asked, holding the grin.

Charlie feigned indignation, "Why, it's a *big secret!*"

"Come on Charlie," Alan coaxed him. "I'll tell you where we're goin', if you tell me your big secret."

"Whall, maybe," Charlie replied. "You first."

Alan looked side-to-side, like he was making sure no one was listening, even though everyone was standing around grinning at his antics. "We're gonna trap the Snake, down Hoback way."

Charlie jumped in mock surprise, "Whall, if that ain't the co-incidence! That was *my* big secret. Me, Bullfrog, and Hugo was just sayin', we're gonna trap the Snake, down the Hoback. We'll be neighbors."

Everyone in the group joined into the joke, and all proclaimed they had planned on trapping that very same area.

George gave his brother a punch in the shoulder, "Stupid, you told 'em. Now, everyone's goin' down there, because they know pa knows the best places. You can't be my brother no more."

"Oh, please, let me be your brother again," Alan pleaded in mock despair. "I won't ever tell Charlie a secret again. I promise."

The group laughed.

Travis shook his head, as he looked over the men, "See what I have to put up with!"

Charlie leaned into George, "Yuh kin be his brother again, we ain't really trappin' down thar."

"Oh, okay," George replied. He looked at Alan, "You can be my brother again. Charlie apologized.

"I did no such thing!" Charlie came back.

Travis held up his hand, "Before this gets any deeper, I think we need to break camp, and go skin some beaver."

The men all agreed, and headed back for their camps to pack out.

By noon, the horses were packed, and camp broke. They all said their good byes, and swore to meet again at rendezvous, wherever the 1829 rendezvous was to be held.

Coon Eyes Charlie, Bullfrog Kincade, and Hugo Montgomery, rode south for Wind River, and the Popo Agie. Warren Gentry and Two Toes Kelly were going back to the South Fork of the Platte. Aaron Dix and Short-leg Jones were headed for the Knife River, maybe meet up with Knife River Mike, and Stinker Willy. Enoch and Billy Coleman were going back to the Green.

The last to leave was Travis and his boys, and Wiley Thompson who stood with them. He gestured toward his partner who was tying down the load on the pack horse, "That Bridger kid is really makin' a name for himself out here. Sharp kid, doesn't miss anything, got a mind like a beaver trap, recalls everything, more nerve than any two men. Can't write, or read, a word, but he's got more in his head than most educated folks I've met. He'll do to take along."

Travis nodded, "He learned a lot from that Hugh Glass mess. Left Glass to die, but he was just a green kid, with a lot to learn about the creed. He learned it though, now he's one of the best men out here. A great tale teller, but true to his word."

"Well, we all make mistakes when we're comin' up," Wiley said. "If every bad thing we ever did was held against us, none of us could stand up straight again."

"Amen to that. You took him under your wing and taught him. You're good for him," Travis said.

"He's a great friend," Alan said. "One day he's gonna make big tracks in this country."

"Come on, Jim," Wiley called out. "We want to catch at least one beaver before rendezvous."

"Hold on ta yer britches, old man," Jim called back. "If all you kin ketch is one beaver before rendezvous, then I picked myself a pitiful partner."

Wiley snorted, "I picked *you*, youngster. Actually, I drew the short straw and got stuck with you."

"Oh, in that case, I'll go with Alan and George, they're my friends," Jim said.

"You're stuck with me, kid, let's go," Wiley said.

"Where are you headed?" Travis asked.

"North Fork. Maybe head over into the Poudre valley and check on Nels and Jimmy. See how they come through the winter."

"We might make our way over there ourselves," Travis said. "We trapped the Poudre the year before they built the cabin in there. Good country."

Jim shook hands with Alan and George, who had all

become fast friends. At twenty-three years of age, the brothers were only three years younger than Bridger. "You boys hold tight to yer topknots," Jim said.

"You watch yours," Alan said back.

Wiley put his hand out to Travis, "You be careful, Big Walker. Expect to see you at rendezvous, you and those boys of yours."

Travis shook his hand, "We'll be there." He then shook Jim's hand, "Don't let him teach you any bad habits."

"Too late," Jim said with a grin.

Travis, Alan, and George stepped into their saddles. Travis gave them a wave, "See you boys at rendezvous."

TRAVIS and the boys settled into a camp where the Hoback River met the Snake. They spent April trapping hard. They worked the Hoback, Snake, and several smaller creeks and streams within the area. Nearing the end of the month, Travis was checking traps on the Snake, south of the river junction.

He was on a hill overlooking the river, when he spotted a saddled horse standing by one of his traps. Looking past the horse, he could see a man pulling his trap out of the water. The thief's back was to him and he couldn't see who it was, but Luther Monk was a notorious fur thief, and suspected in more than one murder for pelts. It was either Monk, or Jory Adams, another outlaw. He was called

Rattlesnake Adams, for his vile nature, and criminal ways. Monk was called a lot of names that were not repeatable in front of women or children.

The hill was steep, and he didn't want to charge the horse down it, taking the chance of its tripping and rolling them both to their deaths. He estimated the fur thief to be about two-hundred yards away. It was a long shot, but if he tried to ride down to the man, he would be gone, with the beaver, before he got there.

Quickly dismounting, he sat down with his rifle, placed a cap on the nipple, took aim on the thief who was in the process of opening the trap jaws to remove the beaver, and pulled the trigger. It was a second before the man stiffened, and jerked upright. He clasped a hand over the small of his back, jumped around in a circle, then ran for his horse. As he mounted, Travis could see that it was Luther Monk. Monk got in the saddle and galloped the horse for the cover of the trees.

Pulling the second rifle from the scabbard, he capped it, took aim at Monk, but then he was gone from sight. Loading the first rifle he slipped them both back into their scabbards. Mounting his horse, he worked his way down the hill, to where Monk had been.

Reaching the trap lying on the bank, a drowned beaver firmly clamped in the jaws, he stopped and looked around. There was no point in chasing Monk, he was gone. No doubt, Monk had been watching him run the traps, that's how he knew where it was. In that case,

Monk knew the trap was his, and he would lay low for a while, but he knew now Travis Walker would kill him if they met again.

He removed the beaver, reset the trap, and rode back toward their camp. Reaching camp, he found Alan and George had returned from running the other lines. He tossed the beaver down on the ground. "How did you do?" Travis asked them.

"Got two," Alan said. "Think we got about all we can from here. Time to move on."

Travis nodded, "Yeah. I just got the one today. Almost lost it though."

"Why? What happened?" George asked.

"I was up on the hill, overlooking the river, and there was Luther Monk pulling the trap out of the water. It was a good two-hundred yards, but I could tell he was taking a beaver out of it. It was too far, and steep, to run him down, so I took a shot at him. Hit him in the back, but not so bad that he couldn't get on his horses, and light a shuck out as fast as he could."

"What is that weasel doin' over here?" George asked. "I thought the Green was his thievin' area."

"Too many trappers on the Green, now," Travis replied. "Too easy to get caught, he has to go elsewhere. So, we got him, but he'll remember me, with that ball in his back. Don't mess with Travis Walker!"

"Did you go after him?" Alan asked.

"Wasn't worth my time," Travis replied. I got the trap

and beaver, and he got shot for his trouble. Figured to leave it there, but if I see him again, I'll beat his ears off."

BY MAY, the animals were shedding their winter coats as the days grew warmer. The trapping ended with a good collection of beaver, in addition to muskrat, mink, otter, fox, and coyote pelts. They would do well at the rendezvous this year.

Come July they began to work their way back up the Snake River, looking for other trappers who would know where the rendezvous was going to be held. Riding into Jackson's Hole at the end of July, they came on Enoch Rose and Billy Coleman camped alongside the river.

Enoch waved at them, "Big Walker, come join us." He laughed, "You can bring those greenhorn kids with yuh."

"Who you callin' *greenhorn*," Alan called back at him. "I've been in the mountains for a whole day. I'm a by-God, mountain man now!"

"Watch your mouth, son," Travis said to him. "Your mother woulda washed your mouth out with soap for blasphemy."

Alan looked up toward Heaven, "Sorry, Ma."

Dismounting, they walked into the camp. Billy stood up, "From the looks of that pack of pelts, I'd say you done well."

Travis dismounted, "We did pretty good. Not as good as a few years back, but good."

"More trappers now," Billy said.

"That's for sure," Travis agreed. "Need some new areas." He, and the boys, led the horses to the river to drink. Then, stripped the saddles and packs off, and staked them out to graze.

Returning to the camp, Travis asked, "Gettin' kind of late in the summer, hear anything about the rendezvous?"

"They just had one on the Popo Agie," Enoch replied.

"What! We missed it?" Travis exclaimed.

Enoch held his hand up, "Easy, Big Walker. Sublette made a stop on the Popo Agie and traded with the trappers gathered there. We got the word from Coon Eyes Charlie, they traded there, but Sublette was movin' on to Pierre's Hole 'cuz there's a bunch of trappers waitin' for him up thar, too."

Travis let out a sigh of relief. "Enoch, you could have started with that, instead of givin' me a heart attack."

Enoch grinned, "Sorry. We're headin' up to Pierre's Hole. Sublette won't get there for a few more days."

"So, we missed the rest of the boys?" Travis asked.

"Yeah, appears that way."

"That's too bad, it would have been fun."

"Charlie figured they'd winter up on the Yellastone again. We'll meet up thar."

Travis nodded, "That's a good place."

TRAVIS AND THE BOYS, along with Enoch and Billy, arrived in Pierre's Hole to find a collection of nearly two-hundred trappers waiting for the pack animals to arrive. Most were camped in the area of Teton Creek. The lodges of the Flatheads stretched out along a creek flowing from north to south on the eastern side of the valley. Riding further up the valley they found the lodges of the Nez Perce set up along the Teton River.

Travis knew some of the trappers who were camped, others were company men, who had stayed over the winter trapping, and waiting for the owners with supplies to come back. Riding by one camp, he spotted the Grant brothers, Morgan and Ben, sitting by their fire. Stopping, Travis called out to them, "Mind if we join you?"

Ben stood up, "Hello, Travis! Haven't seen you in a coon's age. Come on in."

"We wintered on the Yellowstone, and then did our spring trappin' down the Snake," Travis replied.

Morgan walked up beside his brother, and said with a grin, "I see you kept the boys."

Travis laughed, "I can't seem to shake 'em, no matter how hard I try."

"We hang onto his coattails, 'cause we'd get lost if he didn't guide us," Alan said.

Morgan looked past Travis, "Who's that comin' up behind you?"

Travis turned to see Enoch and Billy catching up to them.

"Why, it's Enoch Rose, and Billy Coleman," Morgan said to his brother.

"We might as well make it a party," Ben said. "All of you come on in."

That night in the camp, the men got to discussing the number of trappers that had come in, and their ill-effect on the beaver trapping.

"We're lookin' for a new area," Travis said. "We've trapped pretty much every stream from the North Fork of the Platte, to the Yellowstone. Don't want to go any further north into Blackfoot country. All of the places we trapped over the past six years now have someone else workin' 'em."

"I heard, there's good beaver to the south, yet," Morgan said.

"How far south?" Travis asked. "We've trapped the Poudre Canyon already, but Nels and Jimmy are in there now. Not room enough for two outfits in there."

"How did you go into the Poudre?" Ben asked.

"From the north, off the Laramie plains," Travis answered.

Ben shook his head, "Not there. What I heard was down the South Fork of the Platte. All the way down to the Medicine Bow mountains. Lots of streams and beaver, yet. All the company trappers have been let off on the Green. No one that I know of has gone that far south."

"How did you find out about it, then?" Travis asked.

"Talk along the trail," Ben said. "A few men have gone down to the Spanish lands, and come back. They mentioned the country looks ripe for beaver, but they were explorin' for trails, not trappin'."

"What Indians are down that way?" George asked.

"That's Cheyenne, and 'Rapaho country," Enoch answered.

"Are they friendly, or villains?"

"Not so friendly," Enoch said. "Yuh have to be careful with 'em."

"But, they're children compared to the Blackfeet," Morgan said. "If you can survive the Blackfeet, then the Cheyenne are nothin'."

"I know the Crow don't like 'em," Travis said. "They're about as bad as the Sioux for trespassin'. Still, we need some new country if we're to make anything trappin'." He looked at the boys, "What do you think? After we trade here, head down that way, take a look?"

"We wouldn't have any friends, if we go down there," George said. "Should we run into problems, there's no one to help."

"We didn't have no one to help us when we first came into this country," Alan countered. "We got by."

"We might meet some other trappers down there, and form an alliance," Travis said. "Like Alan said, we didn't know anyone when we first got here. We made all our friends over the years. It could be the same down in the Medicine Bow country."

George stared into the fire, "I don't know, pa, I got a feelin' about it. I don't know."

"I'll tell you what," Travis said. "Let's just ride down that way, and scout it out. If we don't like it, and you still have a bad feelin', we'll come back up this way."

"We should at least have a look," Alan said. "We can come back up here to winter with our friends. All the rendezvous are up here, so we'd have to come back here anyway."

Travis coaxed George, "Let's just give it a look. We might take a ton of beaver out of some untrapped streams."

George nodded, "Okay, but if it doesn't feel right, I wanna come back north."

"We'll do that," Travis agreed. "I promise."

SUBLETTE ARRIVED A FEW DAYS LATER. The Walkers traded their pelts. Then, Travis traded some gunpowder, rifle balls, and his horse to a Nez Perce for a blue roan Palouse stud. Then, they headed south, bound for the South Platte.

Several days later they crossed the North Fork of the Platte, where it split off with the South Fork. Following the South Fork, they knew this was Gentry's and Kelly's area, however, they didn't see them. They entered the Laramie plains, keeping a sharp eye out for Cheyenne, but as of yet had not encountered any.

The land ran flat, with sparse ground cover, save for grass, and a scattering of trees. In the distance, the Medicine Bow mountains rose up above the plains. It was still early morning when they reached the upper fork of the Laramie River. The beaver sign was enough to warrant further scouting.

"Let's spend the day here, and do some scoutin'," Travis said.

"Yeah," Alan agreed, "beaver all over this country. Wonder why no one's come down here?"

"Most of the trappers comin' in now are company men," Travis answered. "They've never been out here, and go where they're told to go. Most are dropped off on the Green. Those we know, are happy with their usual grounds."

"They're missin' out," Alan said. "But, that leaves more for us."

"That's what we're lookin' for," Travis replied. "Let's set up for the day, and night, in those cottonwoods, and do some lookin' around. In the morning we'll keep goin' south, but we might want to work some of this, too."

"I wanna scout down the river," Alan said.

"Okay. You and George stay together, and keep an eye out for the Cheyenne. We haven't seen 'em, yet, but they can come out of nowhere. There's a feeder creek I'm goin' to check out, and see if I can't shoot us some fresh meat. Be back here in two hours."

Both boys agreed to return within the time frame Travis had set.

Alan and George rode down the river, while Travis, not wanting to leave the pack horse and supplies behind, took them with him.

The fur sign on the creek kept Travis moving further along, until he realized he was closing in on the two-hour time he had told the boys to follow. Spotting a herd of deer, he shot a yearling. Gutting the deer, he threw it over the pack load, and headed back for the camp site.

Reaching the campsite, he found the boys still gone. He hung the deer from a tree branch, and unpacked the load. Taking the horses to water, he let them drink. He looked up at the sun, it had been well past two-hours since they left. He knew the boys got carried away when trapping, and often forgot the time, but he was getting concerned.

Tying the horses to the trees, he loosened the cinch on the roan, but didn't unsaddle him. He chose not to start a fire to prevent the smoke from making his location known. When another hour passed, he couldn't wait any longer. Pulling the cinch tight on the roan, he mounted and headed down the river.

As he rode, he saw the tracks left by his sons' horses, but they were not in sight. Half an hour from the place they started, the noisy rasping of ravens and crows gathering in the cottonwoods caught his attention. Scavenger birds gathered, fighting and squawking, when there was something to eat. The fear of what he would find began to choke him.

On the flat plain he saw a body with things sticking out of it. He heeled the horse moving him quickly forward. To his horror, it was Alan completely riddled with arrows. He cried out, as he leaped from the saddle and fell on his knees beside his dead son. He cried out in pain and desperation as he snapped the wretched arrows out of his body. There were twenty, he counted them, but had no idea why. Alan was also scalped. He pulled Alan's limp body against his chest and wept.

In the midst of his nightmare, he realized that George was not there, nor were the horses, their guns, or anything. He would not have left his brother. The Indians had taken George with them, along with stealing everything they had. He needed to go after George, but he couldn't leave Alan for the birds. He lifted Alan and laid him over the saddle, then mounted, sitting back against the cantle. He ran the horse back to the camp.

Laying Alan down, he covered him with a blanket to keep the birds off. Then, stepped back into the saddle, and galloped back to where he had found Alan. He picked up the trail of numerous unshod horse tracks heading down river. He followed them, keeping a watchful eye ahead.

Seeing the smoke from their fire he rode on. Their horses were scattered out, and the Indians were gathered together laughing. He pulled both rifles, capped them, and rode toward the camp. To his renewed horror, that instantly blossomed into fury, he saw they had George tied to a tree and were shooting arrows into him like he was a target.

In his rage, he kicked the horse into a gallop directly through the clustered Indians. Before they could react, the big roan warhorse had run over two of them. With a rifle in each hand, Travis pointed the bores directly into two Indians, and fired. Jumping from the horse, he dropped the rifles, and pulled both Bowie knives. Furiously shouting mountain man yells, and cursing the murderers, he sliced and tore open the terrified Indians. They ran in circles screaming in a frenzy of fear while Travis ran them down and killed them.

A few jumped on their horses and escaped the raging mountain man. Seeing none remaining, Travis, heaving breathes, and still cursing the Indians, went to George and cut him down. Breaking the arrows out of his body, he put him on the horse, and took him back to the camp.

Reaching the camp, he laid George beside his brother. Covered him with a blanket then, went back to the Cheyenne camp to pick up the trails of the escapees. He had no intention of letting any of the murderers escape. Riding through the demolished camp, he counted fourteen that he had killed in his rage. He didn't even recall killing them, he just did it.

Picking up the trail of several horses, he stayed on the tracks for hours before he spotted two Indians walking their horses. He was a hundred yards behind them, but they never looked back. Stopping the roan, he capped both rifles. Taking aim from the saddle, he fired. The Indian on the left pitched off his horse. The second Indian turned to look, cried out, and kicked his horse, but the second Hawken barked, dropping him hard from the running horse.

Travis rode up to them, to be sure they were dead. The rifle balls had done their work. He saw where two other sets of horse tracks kept going, but he would let them escape to tell the others that a crazy mountain man was coming for them. He swore he would hunt down, and kill, every Cheyenne in the country, if it was the last thing he did.

Returning to his dead sons, he buried them there beside the river, and sat down and wept. The night came over him, but he never noticed it. He neither ate, nor drank, just sat ruing the day he made the decision to come down here. George had expressed his concern, but in his blind lust for beaver pelts, he had ignored him. The price of that blindness, now amounted to a cost beyond measure. He had buried his wife and daughters in Tennessee, and now his sons in the wilderness.

Over the summer, he hunted Cheyenne. He became their terror. He killed them in their camps, he killed them day, or night. They came to live in fear that the crazy white trapper, who had killed so many a so quickly, would find them, and kill them as well. The Cheyenne came to call him, *Háestóhenóéoohe,* Kills Many Quickly.

By the end of summer, he had killed near to thirty Cheyenne, aside from those in the camp. The Cheyenne were afraid to sleep should the avenging trapper, who was possessed of an evil spirit, find them, and kill them. It was Gentry and Kelly, from down on the South Platte, who learned what happened to Alan and George, and Travis' rampage through the Cheyenne tribe. They spread the word among the mountain men.

One fall day, exhausted and weary, his wrath spent, Travis rode to the Missouri River, and followed it down. He didn't want to be in the mountains anymore, he didn't want to talk to another human being ever again. He wanted only solitude, and to live with the guilt, pain, and horrible decision, he had made. Coming onto the deteriorating remains of the old trading fort, Fort Osage, he moved into the house. Here he would stay until he died, living with his nightmares, and regrets.

Made in United States
North Haven, CT
08 June 2024

53396057R00114